THE BULLION TRAIL

THE BULLION TRAIL

by

Ed Hapgood

Dales Large Print Books
Long Preston, North Yorkshire,
BD23 4ND, England.

British Library Cataloguing in Publication Data.

Hapgood, Ed
The bullion trail.

A catalogue record of this book is
available from the British Library

ISBN   978-1-84262-756-3 pbk

First published in Great Britain in 2009 by Robert Hale Ltd.

Copyright © Ed Hapgood 2009

Cover illustration © Gordon Crabb by arrangement with
Alison Eldred

The right of Ed Hapgood to be identified as the author of this
work has been asserted by him in accordance with the
Copyright, Designs and Patents Act, 1988

Published in Large Print 2010 by arrangement with
Robert Hale Limited

Dales Large Print is an imprint of Library Magna Books Ltd.

Printed and bound in Great Britain by
T.J. (International) Ltd., Cornwall, PL28 8RW

For Betty, in loving memory

CHAPTER 1

Three men sat in the office of the Stanhope Bank in Hawkesville. The one was easily identifiable, since he wore the uniform of an army major. The second, too, wore an army uniform, only this time that of a sergeant. The third member was seated behind the only desk in the office – he was the bank manager.

The manager, whose name was Miles, cleared his throat.

'Well, that seems to be satisfactory,' he announced.

The major nodded.

'Yes, we seem to have covered everything.'

'Can I say something?' The third member spoke up.

The other two regarded him with not a little surprise. During the conversation that had just taken place, he had been silent. In fact the other two had almost completely forgotten about his existence. Now here he was obviously bringing up a further point for discussion just when they had assumed that the meeting was over.

'Yes, what is it, Benson?' demanded the major.

'Well, sir, I've got a small reservation about this venture.'

'A small reservation?' The bank manager couldn't have sounded more surprised if the sergeant had said that all the bank's deposits had been stolen.

'What is this small reservation, Benson?' There was a large degree of annoyance in the major's tone, although he never usually allowed a member of the public to see that he was critical of one of his men.

'It's about the publicity.' Benson plunged ahead, ignoring the coldness with which his remark had been greeted.

'What's your point, sergeant?' demanded the bank manager.

'Well, we're transporting one hundred gold bars to Mexico. I'd like to know who will know about it.'

Both men sat back in their chairs while they digested Benson's remark. The bank manager's chair was a comfortable armchair and so he had no problem in leaning back in it. The major, on the other hand, was a large man and his chair had none of the padded opulence of the manager's. So his movement was limited to a small shift of his weight. As an added gesture he folded his arms.

The bank manager obviously decided that the question was aimed at him.

'Apart from us three, there will obviously be the people who will be loading the gold on to the wagon. These will be employees of the bank. I envisage that there will be three of them. Two doing the actual loading, while the third keeps watch.'

'Is there any need for the bank employees to load the gold on to the wagon?'

'What do you mean?' the bank manager

was genuinely puzzled.

'I'd like three men from the regiment to load the gold. We'd take it to the camp. It would cut down the number of people who know about the transfer.'

The manager favoured the sergeant with a condescending smile.

'I appreciate your concern for the safety of the gold, Sergeant. But I can assure you that the three members of the bank whom I have chosen to load the gold have been with us for a considerable number of years.' He re-emphasized the point. 'A considerable number of years. And they are completely trustworthy.'

The major stared at Benson as though expecting him to make a further remark. Benson merely shrugged his shoulders.

The bank manager stood up to indicate that the meeting was over. He shook hands with the major. The two army men were about to leave when the bank manager said: 'Can I have a word with you, Major?'

The major signalled to Benson to go

ahead. When the door was closed behind him, the bank manager said: 'Are you sure you've got the right person for this task? I was expecting somebody of a higher rank.'

'Benson is a completely trustworthy soldier,' said the major. 'I've chosen him because he's the only person in the camp who speaks fluent Spanish. This could be of considerable value when he arrives in Mexico.'

'It's your decision. I hope you're right, Major.' The bank manager's parting remark contained a certain measure of doubt.

CHAPTER 2

The dance in the main hall of the army camp was in full swing. The cavalrymen had little chance to hold a dance and so any excuse was seized upon to hold a function. The reason this time was that ten of their number were going to Mexico on a secret mission.

The band consisted of half a dozen of the cavalrymen who had been given the task of playing for the men and their wives that evening. The drummer was a regimental rarity – someone who had been with the cavalry for twenty years. He had even seen a spell of duty under General Custer. However he had transferred from the ill-fated Seventh Cavalry in time to ensure that he had continued to live and to enjoy his existence as a soldier.

The other members of the band owed their ability to play instruments to the army. The two trumpeters were an essential part of any cavalry charge. These days there was less demand for cavalry charges than in the past, but they performed useful regular tasks such as playing the reveille. And, of course, playing the unenviable 'last post' at a soldier's funeral.

The other three members of the band – the pianist, the violinist and the bass player – had all been instrumentalists before joining the army. But the hope of a more exciting life had brought them into the Eleventh Cavalry and now they were playing for their comrades who were obviously enjoying themselves.

The fact that many of the men had been allowed to bring their wives with them to live on the camp helped to make an occasion like this a success. In addition some of the soldiers had girlfriends, who had come to the camp on the special occasion of a dance. In fact there was no shortage of female companionship for those soldiers who wanted to join in the dance.

As in any dance there were men standing around watching the dancers. Most of them were in small groups. They would pass comments about the dancers, knowing that they were safe from the dancers overhearing them, since their observations would be drowned by the music. This was particularly true of the current dance which happened to be a noisy polka.

The Master of Ceremonies announced that there would be a slight interval and then the next dance would be a waltz. The slight interval meant that the soldiers and the ladies who needed additional refreshments would be able to satisfy their thirst at the bar.

'You haven't danced, Sergeant.'

The observation came from an attractive blonde named Emily, who was only just out of her teens. Had she been older she would have realized that it strictly wasn't etiquette to approach a soldier and pose such a question.

Tom Benson looked down at her.

'Dancing isn't one of my favourite occupations.' With the wisdom which is supposed to come with age the young lady would have recognized the statement as a concealed snub. However, being too young she was not aware of the implied slight, and so Emily plunged on: 'I believe some soldiers aren't dancing because they are nursing some war wound or other.'

'That doesn't apply to me.'

'And, of course others aren't dancing because they feel that going on to floor shows a certain lack of proficiency in a certain dance.'

'So I believe.'

The message finally got through to Emily that the sergeant was not only unapproachable but was only within a hair's breadth of being downright rude in his choice of replies to her.

'If you will excuse me, I will go back to my friends,' she said, more sharply than she intended, turning on her heel.

Why had be been so abrupt with her? She just wanted to be friendly. There was an innocence about her which would have appealed to many men. But not to Tom Benson. Not to somebody who had lost his wife and child when she was in childbirth a few months' back. His refuge had been to get drunk as often as possible afterwards. At that time he had been a captain. But in one of his drunken brawls he had stepped over the line that the army recognizes as acceptable behaviour. The result was that he had been demoted to sergeant.

For the next half hour or so he watched the dancers. Nobody approached him; nobody spoke to him, since he had established himself as a loner after his demotion. When his wife, Carlotta, had been alive they were often the life and soul of the party. She was beautiful, vivacious and witty. In fact their company had been much sought after. They would always be the first to be invited to any party or dance. Now he was standing by the wall, on his own. Which was as it should be since he didn't make any effort to be sociable.

The MC announced the last dance. By a strange coincidence, Emily was standing near him. She was looking around as though searching for somebody. For some unfathomable reason Tom approached her.

'May I have the next dance, please?'

She turned. When she recognized him she regarded him with surprise. She hesitated before replying. When she did speak she saw the hurt on his face.

'I'm sorry. I'm waiting for my partner.'

CHAPTER 3

Ten horsemen were riding towards the river. They were accompanying a covered wagon. The horses which had been going through the desert seemed to quicken their pace automatically although the river was still about four miles ahead. Tom Benson had made sure that the riders had started early – an hour before sunrise. This had brought a few muttered complaints from some of the younger members of the platoon. But the older soldiers had agreed with Tom's decision.

'We should get through the desert before sun begins to burn,' said one of the old cavalrymen. 'If we don't then they'll be able to peel your skin away when you get back to camp.'

Luckily they crossed the twenty mile or so

of desert without mishap. Now they were nearing the river. Tom, who had made the journey several times before, began to relax.

All the cavalrymen were privates with the exception of Tom and another sergeant, Shanklin Drew. He was about the same age as Tom, in his early thirties. He couldn't claim the status of once being a captain. He was not the sort of person Tom would have chosen as a companion – but the choice was the major's. Drew was riding alongside Tom.

'It's good to leave that place behind us,' he stated.

'Yeah,' agreed Tom.

'I've only been to San Caldiz once. I seem to remember it was a pretty lively town.'

'That's right.'

'If I remember there were some very pretty *señoritas* there.'

'I expect there still are,' said Tom, drily.

'We'll have to stay a night. What are your plans?'

'We'll find somewhere to camp.'

'That will mean we should be able to have a few tequilas before we turn in.'

'Somewhere to camp will be just the other side of the river. We've got to start early in the morning to get across the desert. We can't start back from San Caldiz which is six miles from the river. We'd never get across the desert before the sun sapped the strength of the horses.'

'The men won't be happy with that,' observed Drew. 'They were expecting to spend a night in San Caldiz.'

'What they expect and what they get are two different matters,' stated Tom.

They reached the river and the horses joyfully waded in. They began to quench their thirst with the cool water. The soldiers jumped down and they too splashed around happily.

'Don't drink the water,' Tom commanded. 'You should have enough water left in your water-bottles to keep you going until we reach San Caldiz.'

'How far away is that, sir?' asked one of

the older soldiers.

'About six miles,' said Tom.

'If you want to cool off in the river,' Tom addressed the remark to Drew. 'You go ahead.'

'I think I will.' Drew jumped down from his horse and began to splash the water into his face.

Tom was the only one left on his horse. The other two soldiers who hadn't joined those in the river were the two on the wagon.

'All right, you can join them,' said Tom. 'Make sure the brakes are on the wagon.'

The soldiers needed no second invitation. They too jumped down to join the others.

Tom sat in the saddle and surveyed the scene. His mind went back to other occasions when he had sat on the river bank and watched his men splashing in the river. He had travelled back and forth to Mexico on army duties at least a dozen times. Most of the journeys had been uneventful. Then, on one particular occasion, when he was staying in San Caldiz he had met the beautiful Carlotta. It had been a whirlwind romance – it had to be of necessity, since he was only in the town for a few days before he would complete his army business.

The result was that when he had finished that business he had started a new venture. He was married to Carlotta.

They had spent several months of happiness together at the camp. Carlotta had taught some of the wives the intricacies of the Spanish dancing, until she became too plump with a child to do so.

Then one day when he had returned to camp having been out on a patrol, he knew from the faces of his friends that something was wrong. It was the major who broke the news to him.

'I'm afraid, Tom, that I have bad news. Your baby was born prematurely. There were complications. Carlotta and the baby are dead.'

That day something had died inside him. True, he went on living because there was nothing else he could do. But on at least a couple of occasions when the patrols had been attacked by Apaches he had deliberately put himself in extreme danger. His fervent wish was that an Apache bullet would kill him. Then he would join Carlotta.

But it hadn't happened. Now, here he was, six months later, sitting on his horse on the riverbank.

'All right. Get back on your horses,' he shouted. Although he was only a sergeant, he could still command like the officer he had once been, he thought ruefully.

They entered San Caldiz an hour or so later. None of the privates had been there before and they looked around with interest as they rode down the main street. Those who had expected the buildings to reflect the poverty they heard about in Mexico were surprised at some of the elegant houses they passed. In fact their home town of Hawkesville came off second best in comparison to the obvious signs of wealth in many of the buildings.

Tom watched the expressions on some of the faces of the soldiers.

'Not quite what you expected, is it, Blake?' Tom addressed one of the soldiers.

'It certainly isn't. I thought Mexico was a poor country.'

'Most of it is. But some parts of it are very wealthy, as you can see.'

The sidewalks were the same as in America. The main difference was that there seemed to be more people on them. Most of the women were wearing colourful costumes.

'Somebody in the camp said that the *señoritas* here were very beautiful. They were quite right.' The remark came from one of the soldiers named Stickley.

The remark triggered Tom's thoughts about his own beautiful wife and the first time he had seen her. It was on an occasion like this when he had been leading his men into town. The sidewalk had been crowded with sightseers – probably more so than it was now. It had been fiesta week and many people had come into town from the surrounding countryside. The soldiers had been riding along casually when the tragedy occurred. A small child ran in front of the horses. In fact it ran in front of Tom's horse.

He had a split second to try to avoid hitting the child. There was only one thing he could do. He pulled viciously on the reins causing the horse to rear. While the horse was in the air he was aware of the screams of horror from the crowd. The small child had frozen under the horse's front hoofs. When the horse came back down it was inevitable that it would crush the child. There was nothing that Tom could do. The horse had already begun to come back down to earth. Then a miracle happened. A woman dashed out from the crowd. She seized the child. Before the horse came back down to earth she had dived to safety with the child in her arms.

Tom and the riders pulled up. He searched the crowd for the woman who had risked her own safety by seizing the child. But she was nowhere to be seen.

That evening Tom and his men had been the guests of the mayor at the fiesta. Tom was seated next to the mayor on one of the seats reserved for the dignitaries. One of the main items was the bullfight. It obviously enthralled the large audience but it left Tom cold. Especially in the end when the bull was needlessly slaughtered.

The mayor noticed Tom's reaction.

'You do not find bullfights to your taste?'

'It's a good spectacle. But when I see the killing of the bull I think of all the cows on my brother's ranch that that magnificent animal could have sired.'

'You have a point,' said the mayor, with a smile. 'But in its short life the bull has been treated like a king. It has had everything he could desire.'

'The only consolation is he couldn't have known that he was going to have such a horrible ending,' stated Tom.

'Your profession is killing men, yet you are against killing an animal,' observed the mayor.

'There is one thing I must admit,' stated Tom. 'The bullfighter has shown exceptional courage. I would welcome him in my regiment any day.'

The mayor smiled. 'You never know,' he said. 'If you come to see bullfights often enough you will grow to appreciate all the techniques behind the spectacle.'

Tom dismissed the remark as one of the most unlikely occurrences in his life. True he had a few more days to spend in San Caldiz in which he had to inspect and if possible improve the town regiment. He would be staying on while his men would be on their way home the following day. He would prefer to be going home with them since his assignment didn't appeal to him.

How could he improve the town regiment in that time? If what he had seen of some of them who were lining the streets today it would take three months to improve them, not three days.

His thoughts were interrupted by a fanfare. It heralded the arrival of a dancer. Tom was astonished to see that it was the young lady who had saved the young child by rescuing her from in front of his horse. When she started to dance he was immediately captivated by her movements. Suddenly the prospect of staying in San Caldiz, which hadn't appealed to him a few moments ago, now seemed the most desirable way of spending the next few days. He might even watch another bullfight if the exquisite beauty on the stage would be one of the performers.

The mayor, who had been taking almost a fatherly interest in Tom's reactions during the fiesta, could not but notice the way he sat forward in his seat to watch every movement of the dancer.

'Do you appreciate dancing, Captain?'

'When it is so exquisitely performed by such a beauty who couldn't appreciate it?'

'There will be a small reception in my tent at the end of the fiesta. I will introduce you to Carlotta.'

He had introduced them. It was soon

obvious that not only did Tom only have eyes for Carlotta, but that she responded warmly to his attentions. It was what lady novelists call love at first sight, Tom decided ruefully.

They had arrived at the bank. Tom called the platoon to a halt. A Mexican hurried out through the front door.

'I am the bank manager. I will show you the way round the back,' he fussed.

He led them down a lane that was only just wide enough for the wagon. They ended up in a small deserted square. He pointed to a white double door and Tom indicated to the wagon driver to follow the bank manager's instructions.

The wagon came to a halt just outside the door. The bank manager released the padlock and flung open the doors. The assistant in the wagon jumped down and took off the tarpaulin. The soldiers still on their horses watched the proceedings with interest. They were going to see one hundred gold bars being transferred from the wagon to the bank.

Two bank employees had come out from the bank to help to carry the gold. The bullion was in five strong boxes. Tom jumped down from his horse. The bank manager looked at him enquiringly.

'Have you got the key?' he asked in Spanish.

To his surprise Tom answered in the same language.

'Here it is.' He handed the key over.

The bank manager opened the first chest. He stepped back. Not to admire the gold inside, but with an expression of disbelief on his face. The chest held not gold bars, but ordinary house bricks.

Tom was seated in the mayor's office. The mayor was not the same person he had met on his previous visits to San Caldiz. Tom had established a friendly relationship with that mayor, but unfortunately he had died and a younger mayor had replaced him.

There was nothing in this mayor's manner to suggest that he would resume the relationship of his predecessor.

They were seated in an opulent office with the mayor in position behind a large oak desk. The thick Persian carpet on the floor helped to give the room its refined air and reminded any visitor that its owner, if not a royal personage, was not too far down the ladder in the scale of importance.

The mayor had introduced himself as Fernando when Tom had been brought to him a few minutes before. He had the swarthy complexion of many of his compatriots, with sleek black hair and a small moustache. His narrow face, small eyes and rather thin lips completed a face which few would describe as handsome. At the moment the lips were twisted in an expression of disbelief.

'You say that one hundred gold bars have vanished.'

'Well, not exactly vanished,' corrected Tom. 'I'm sure there's an explanation.'

The mayor rose from his desk. He went

over to the large window and looked out. Tom knew that his platoon were in the courtyard below awaiting his orders to move on.

'The bank manager assures me that the gold was an important agreement between our bank and your bank in Texas. Not only was it important because of its value but also because it set the seal on the growing friendship between our two countries. A friendship which unfortunately had been allowed to deteriorate in the past.'

'I'm sure he's right,' said Tom. Inwardly he thought why doesn't he come to the point and let us go back to the camp. We're wasting time. The sooner I can get back the sooner I can start an investigation into what has happened to the gold.

'You were the only person who had the keys to the chests, I believe.'

'That's right.'

'Did you open any of the chests before you started in order to check that the gold was inside?'

'No, I didn't think it necessary. We had to start early to get across the desert.'

'Ah, yes, the desert.' The mayor resumed his seat. 'Of course with hindsight it would have been the correct thing to do to see whether the gold was in the chests,' pursued the mayor.

'Yes, I suppose so.' Tom didn't add that after the dance on the previous night everyone was feeling a little worse for wear. At some other time when there had been no party on the previous night he probably would have given at least one of the chests a cursory inspection. But this morning there had been no such inspection.

'Have you any idea who stole the gold?'

'No, none at all.'

'It must have been well planned.'

'Yes.'

'With someone – as they say in your country – on the inside to provide the robbers with the information.'

'It seems like it.'

'It seems like it.' The mayor repeated

Tom's statement while staring at him as though he were trying to memorize his face.

'I'll have to report the theft to the bank in Hawkesville.'

'One hundred gold bars. It's a lot of gold,' said the mayor, thoughtfully.

'The sooner I can get back, the sooner we can start looking for them.'

'What will happen if you don't find them?'

'That's up to the bank.'

'It makes us all look rather foolish.' The mayor stroked his moustache.

It was the sort of remark that didn't warrant a reply. Tom kept silent.

'Particularly you, if I may say so, Sergeant.'

Again it was a remark that didn't need any reply.

'If the gold is found – or replaced – would you convey a message to your commanding officer.'

'Certainly.'

'Tell him the next time he sends any delivery of anything valuable, to choose a person to deliver it who is more efficient. And preferably someone who is of a suitable rank to take charge of such a delivery.'

The mayor rang a small bell to indicate that the interview was over.

CHAPTER 4

The soldiers' return to the camp was unusual because it was conducted in silence. Normally there would be some comments passed to and fro among the men. But not on this occasion. The silence was observed even in the journey through the desert.

They arrived back in the camp just as darkness was closing in. Apart from the sentries on duty everybody was inside the barracks. Tom knew that he had one of the most unpleasant tasks in front of him that he would ever be called upon to perform in the army.

He knocked on the major's door and received the usual command to enter. The major had a welcoming smile on his face. It was the sort of smile which said, give me the expected news that everything went according to plan.

'Well, Tom?'

Tom's hesitation should have warned the major that something was amiss. But whether he had had a tiring day and was on the point of turning in for the night, or whether he wasn't fully concentrating on the sergeant in front of him – whatever the reason, in the first instance he missed Tom's hesitation.

Eventually, though, when Tom hadn't replied to his leading question it did begin to dawn on him that something was amiss. His eyes narrowed and a frown appeared on his forehead. It was a sure sign that he was troubled about something. Tom hadn't been a soldier on the camp for eight years without being able to read the sign clearly.

'Well?' This time the word was delivered in a sharper tone.

'We didn't deliver the gold.'

'Why not?'

'Because it had been stolen and ordinary building bricks had been put in its place.'

Tom was on the receiving end of much the

same stare that he had been subjected to from the mayor of San Caldiz.

'The gold had been stolen?' asked the major, slowly.

'That's right. Either it was stolen before the bank delivered it here, or it was stolen while it was here in our care.'

'It couldn't have been stolen while it was here,' snapped the major. 'We've got guards on the gate.'

'Then it must have been stolen when it was being transferred from the bank.' Tom was relieved that at least they were discussing the theft like reasonable human beings. He reasoned that the worst was over.

'If we assume that somebody stole the money while it was still in the possession of the bank, then it can't be our responsibility,' said the major, thoughtfully.

Better and better, assumed Tom. Maybe at any moment he would soon be dismissed and be able to go to his room and stretch out on his bunk. It had been a tiring day.

'Wait a minute,' said the major. 'You

checked the chests before you set out. What was in them then?'

It was the question that Tom was dreading.

'I didn't check them, sir.' Why had his mouth become unaccountably dry?

'You – didn't – check – them?' There was a dramatic pause between each word that would have done justice to any stage actor.

'I didn't think there was any need.' Tom elaborated on his previous statement.

The major stroked his chin. It was a sure sign that he was deep in thought.

Tom stood to attention. The silence became unbearable. Finally the major spoke.

'I want you in this room at ten o'clock. It's too late to go into the matter tonight.'

A relieved Tom saluted and left the room.

It was ten minutes to ten the following morning when Tom was standing outside the door. He hadn't gone into the dining-room to have his usual breakfast. He knew he would have had to face a sea of enquiring faces. So he had stayed in his room. He had polished his boots with extra thoroughness and cleaned his buttons until they shone. Now he had to wait for the next ten agonizing minutes to pass.

They passed as slowly as an old man with a stick. With a huge effort he managed to refrain from looking at his watch. The major's room was at the end of a corridor and nobody passed him while he was waiting. Tom was dimly aware of the soldiers as they drilled outside on the parade ground.

He tried not to think what form any punishment could take. But the thought kept surfacing regularly like a diver coming up for air. In the end he was forced to examine the most likely punishment. The one that persisted and stayed in his mind, refusing to budge, was that he would lose one of the stripes. He would be demoted to a corporal. It would be an undignified demotion. But he would have to bear it. After all, he had been demoted once before, so the process was not new to him. Of course the demotion would mean that he would receive less pay. But since he didn't have a family to support, it wouldn't make too much difference.

He finally checked his watch. One minute to ten. He took a deep breath and knocked on the door.

If Tom had wished to keep secret the punishment he had received his wish was shattered when a few minutes later the major spelled it out in a loud voice. Indeed the major's voice was loud enough to be heard on the parade ground. The recruits stopped drilling in order to listen to the major's shouted remarks.

'Your punishment is that you are cashiered from the regiment. You will hand in your uniform. You will not come near the camp in future. You will collect your last payment and any personal belongs which you have. You can consider your career in the army to be terminated as from this moment.'

An hour later Tom was leaving the camp for the last time. It had been easy to say farewell

44

to his close friends, since he had none. After the death of Carlotta he had not mixed with anyone. He had become a loner, and once the others in the regiment realized that fact, they had observed his desire to be left alone.

He had changed into his civilian suit, reflecting as he did so that there had been no need for him to have polished the buttons on his army suit so painstakingly. Then he had visited the store sergeant. He had handed over his army uniform, his pistol and his sword.

The sergeant, whose name was Weller, was an elderly man who had been in the army many years longer than Tom.

'I'm sorry, Tom, that things turned out like this,' Weller remarked.

'Yeah, thanks. I suppose it's the luck of the draw,' replied Tom.

The parade ground was deserted when Tom started to walk across it. The recruits who had been training earlier were out on manoeuvres. However Tom knew that there were at least a dozen pairs of eyes – most of them officers' and sergeants' – who were inside the barracks watching him.

He completed the long walk across the parade ground and turned towards the stables. The person in charge, a corporal named Laidlow, hadn't heard the major's speech when he had dismissed Tom and so wasn't aware of Tom's dismissal from the army.

'So you want Chinook today?' asked Laidlow.

'No, not today,' replied Tom. He approached the horse who nuzzled him affectionately. They had been together for three years and there was the usual strong bond of affection which was formed between a cavalryman and his horse.

'I'll give him a good rub down,' said Laidlow.

'Yes, you do that,' said Tom, giving the horse his usual present of an apple.

As he walked away from the stables, Tom felt the first pang of emotion about leaving the camp. It had taken his horse to stir any sense of loss inside him. In fact he felt quite choked at the thought that he would never see Chinook again.

He went through the gates and the sentries gave him the customary wave. They, too, hadn't heard about his dismissal from the army.

Outside the gate he was surprised to see a pony and trap. He was even more surprised when the young girl inside said: 'Can I give you a ride into town?'

Tom stared up at her. Where had he seen her before? Suddenly it came to him: she was the girl at the dance. The one who had turned him down when he had asked her to dance with him.

'It's all right. I'm walking.'

He started in the direction of Hawkesville.

'Why are you always rude?'

She was keeping pace with him in the trap.

'I wasn't aware that I am.'

'You were rude to me the night of the dance, and now you are refusing my help.'

'I've told you I'm quite capable of walking.'

'I'm sorry that you had to leave the army. But there's no need to take it out on me.'

'How did you know that I had to leave the army.'

'I couldn't help overhearing. Everybody heard Uncle Stanley shouting at you.'

'The major is your uncle?' Tom stopped with surprise. She pulled up the trap as well.

'That's right. If you'll jump up, I'll explain all about my family background.'

Tom still hesitated.

'Oh, come on,' she coaxed. 'Don't be so stuffy.'

Maybe it was her choice of the word stuffy. Or maybe it was the fact that she really was attractive. Whatever the reason, Tom didn't stop to analyse it. He jumped up on to the trap.

'My name is Emily Gibbs, and yours is Tom Benson. There, the introductions are over,' she said, as she flicked the horse with her whip to make it start.

'So the major is your uncle,' said Tom, slowly.

'That's right. My parents died when I was a young girl. I was brought up by my aunt and uncle. Probably the reason why you haven't seen me around the camp is that they sent me to a finishing school in England. I've been there for the last four years.'

'Now that you've come back, what do you intend doing?'

'Not me. Them.'

'I don't understand.'

She faced him. 'Uncle Stanley and Aunt Matilda intend finding me a husband.'

'Ah, I see.' There was a slight smile on Tom's face.

'I don't think it's funny,' she snapped. 'They might as well put an advertisement in the paper. Twenty-year-old female fit for marriage. Has all her teeth. Has a good complexion. Is still a virgin. Can sing, play the piano and has all the social graces of a well-brought-up young lady,' she concluded bitterly.

'And is pretty,' Tom added.

'That's a nice thing to say,' she studied

49

him and almost drove the trap off the road.

'Hey! Watch where you're going.' Tom grabbed the reins and for a moment their hands were on the reins together. She drew away and began to concentrate on the road.

'You've heard my history. Now what about you?'

Tom sighed. 'You know about me losing my wife and child.'

'Yes, I'm sorry about that.'

'There's not a lot more to add. I've been cashiered. I'll probably get drunk for a week then go to my brother's ranch. It's a few hundred miles east of here.'

'Do you fancy the idea of being a farmer.'

'No,' said Tom, shortly.

There was a long pause. Emily said finally, 'I don't think it's fair. Making you take the blame for losing the gold.'

It was Tom's turn to subject her to a long stare. She really was a pretty young thing. 'In this world, young Emily,' he said, 'you'll often find that things happen which you wouldn't consider to be fair.'

CHAPTER 5

A quarter of an hour later Tom was in the Stanhope bank. Emily had dropped him off just outside the bank at his request. Her parting words were, 'Take care, Tom,' before giving him a parting kiss.

In the bank Tom approached the counter. There were two assistants working there. He assumed that the manager was in the back room where he had met with him a few days' earlier. Both cashiers were fairly young men in their late twenties. One of them was serving a customer so Tom approached the other.

'I don't have an account here,' said Tom. 'But I'd like to open one.'

'Certainly,' said the cashier, giving Tom a welcoming smile. 'How much money would you like to deposit?'

'Two hundred dollars,' replied Tom. He hadn't spent much money since Carlotta had died. It meant that he had saved up most of his pay. He had received the two hundred dollars savings and thirty dollars more from the pay sergeant when he had left the camp.

'If you could just fill in this form.' The cashier handed Tom a form.

Tom studied it. 'I can't fill in the details of my address. I'm planning to find lodgings in Hawkesville, but I haven't found any yet.'

'That's all right, sir. Have you got the money with you?'

'Yes.'

'Then I'll give you a receipt for it, if you'll fill in your name. Then when you've found lodgings you can call back here. I'll have made up a bank book for you, which you can collect when you call in.'

Tom wrote his name on the form then waited while the cashier counted out the money.

'Right, that's all in order,' he said, putting

the notes in a drawer. 'It's been nice doing business with you, Mr Benson.'

'Thank you, Mr–'

'Fletchley. When you've found lodgings come in for your bank book.'

Tom stepped outside the bank. Although the army camp was only a couple of miles from the town, he had actually spent very little time in Hawkesville. When Carlotta had been alive they had attended a few of the town's functions. Mostly they were dances organized by the mayor. At that time he had been a captain and so had met many of the dignitaries of the town. How it had all changed! They wouldn't want to recognize him now, he reflected, as he headed for the nearest saloon, the Lucky Strike.

During the years that he had been in the army the number of saloons in Hawkesville had grown considerably. He wasn't sure how many there had been when he was a raw recruit but it was only a handful. Now there were twenty-four. That showed the success of a town – when the number of saloons could increase as it had.

There were only half a dozen regulars in the bar. Tom ordered a beer from the barman who, from his swarthy complexion, looked as though he had more than a little Mexican blood in his veins. While he was slowly drinking his beer Tom came to a decision.

'Have you got any rooms to let?' he demanded.

'Sure.' The barman flashed him a smile.

'Right. I'll take one.'

'How long do you think you'll be staying?'

'I'm not sure. For a few days at least.'

The barman produced a battered register.

'If you will sign the book, my wife will show you up to your room.'

Tom signed his name. The barman turned the register around in order to read it. Tom, who was watching his reaction could have sworn that there was a start of surprise on the barman's face when he examined the name.

So the news about him being cashiered had already spread to the town, Tom decided, as Maria led him up the stairs to his room. Well, they said that news travelled fast in the territory, especially bad news.

'Here you are, Mr Benson.'

If there had been any doubt about the existence of Mexican blood in the barman's ancestry, there was certainly none about his wife. She was a plump Mexican with a ready smile.

The room was adequate. It had a bed, a wardrobe, and a chest of drawers on which was a large washing jug.

'I'll bring some water and towels,' she fussed.

'Thank you, Maria. I'd like a meal whenever you can arrange for it.'

'I'll have a steak ready for you in half an hour. Do you like Mexican food? Tortillas and chilli?'

'I love Mexican food,' said Tom.

Maria's huge smile told him that his answer had made him a friend for life.

After having a wash Tom strolled down to the bar. The barman called out to him.

'Mr Benson. Maria says that your meal will be ready in ten minutes. It's in the dining-room – through the door and on your left.'

'Thanks, um–'

'Santos.'

'I'll have a beer while I'm waiting.'

Maria's meal turned out to be the best that Tom had eaten for ages. His evident enjoyment brought a smile to Maria's face.

'Are you sure the chilli wasn't too hot? Next time I could make it cooler.'

'It was just perfect. I've lived in Mexico and I love the food.'

After the meal Tom retired to the bar. A group of noisy cowboys had entered while he had been having his meal. Tom stood by the corner of the bar. He ordered a whiskey while idly watching the cowboys who were engaged in a noisy game of quoits.

He had drunk several whiskeys when one of the cowboys called across to him.

'Hey, mister, would you like to join in? A dollar a throw.'

'All right, I'll have a game,' replied Tom.

One of the other cowboys spoke up.

'It's all right, he'll be playing with a silver dollar. If it was a gold coin he would probably lose it.'

The bar erupted into laughter.

Tom awoke with a splitting headache. It took him a few seconds to realize that he was in bed. Who had put him to bed, and why was he still wearing his clothes? It took him a few seconds longer to realize that he wasn't in bed in his room in the saloon, but in jail. The bars a few feet away provided the vital clue.

He tried to rise to his feet from the bunk. It sent daggers of pain through his head. As a form of exercise rising from a bed should be comparatively easy. But not when you've been hit from behind with the butt of a revolver. Because that's what Tom assumed had happened to him.

Although his head was aching abominably his brain was working clearly. He remembered the outburst of laughter when one of the cowboys had said that he could join in the game of quoits as long as he played with a silver dollar. If he had played with a gold coin he would probably have lost it. He remembered landing a punch on the cowboy's jaw. For a second he'd had the satisfaction of seeing the cowboy sink to the floor. Then everything went blank. Because one of the other cowboys had hit him with his revolver.

Tom moved slowly and deliberately so that he ended up sitting on the edge of his bunk. There, that hadn't been too bad. Maybe in a few hours he could take the bull by the horns and try to stand up.

He looked round the cell. As cells go it had a pretty standard appearance. Not that he was an expert in their construction, since the only other time he had spent in one had been as a guest of the army. It had been as a result of one of his hell-raising exploits when he had been trying to come to terms with Carlotta's death. On that particular occasion he and a few drunken comrades had tried their best to wreck a saloon by shooting at all the bottles on the shelf behind the bar. He had been the one who had been chosen as the sacrificial lamb – partly because of his rank as a captain.

So he had ended up in a cell much the same as this. His punishment at that time had been to lose his status as a captain and become demoted to a sergeant. He wondered what form his punishment would take this time.

How long had he been unconscious? He checked his watch. The movement started his head aching again. It ached even more when he tried the simple calculation of deducting the time he had been hit over the head from the time at present. He eventually came up with the answer. Two hours. He had been unconscious for two hours.

He had just arrived at this conclusion when there was the sound of footsteps along the corridor. A thin young man appeared who was identified by his deputy badge.

'The sheriff wants to see you,' he announced.

'Have you been here before to see whether I'd recovered,' demanded Tom, as he rose slowly to his feet.

'Twice,' replied the deputy.

Tom was led to the sheriff's office where an overweight sheriff sat behind his desk. He was in his early forties and his unhealthy pink complexion suggested that he was not averse to a regular drink of whiskey.

'Sit down, Benson,' he indicated the only other chair in the office. 'It's all right, you can go, I'll deal with this.' He addressed the remark to the deputy who obediently left the office.

'I want to know why I was brought here,' said Tom. 'Why wasn't I taken up to my room in the saloon?'

'You started a fracas,' said the sheriff, whose name was Sankey.

'I might have lashed out at one of the cowboys, but one of the others overreacted by hitting me unconscious. He should have been in the cell, not me.'

'Are you trying to teach me my job?'

Sankey's lips were set in an unattractive scowl.

'What's happened to the guy who hit me?'

'He's one of the Bar T cowboys. I've dealt with him. He won't be coming into town for the next few weeks. That's the worst punishment a cowboy can receive.'

'I know worse punishments,' snapped Tom.

'Let me make this plain,' said Sankey. 'I think you're a troublemaker. We don't like troublemakers in Hawkesville. There's only one reason why I don't put you back in your cell.'

'The reason is because you'd have to charge me with disturbing the peace. And you know you'd never make it stick.'

'You think you're clever, don't you? Well we don't like clever people who cause trouble in this town. So I'm giving you twenty-four hours to get out. If you're still here at the end of that time, you will taste our hospitality again in your cell. Is that clear? That's all.'

Tom stood up. He walked slowly to the door.

'By the way,' the sheriff called out after him. 'If you're wondering what the one reason is why you're not going back to your cell it's because you're not carrying a gun.'

Tom made his way slowly back to the saloon. If the sheriff was as good as his word he only had twenty-four hours to try to find out what had happened to the gold. It sounded like an impossible task.

On his way to the saloon he had to pass the bank. It was obvious that it was closing since one of the assistants had just finished locking the window shutter. As Tom approached he could see that it was Fletchley, the assistant he had seen earlier. It was obvious that he recognized Tom.

'Your bank book is ready, if you would like it now, Mr Benson.'

It didn't matter to Tom whether he would collect it now or not. Especially since he would probably be leaving Hawkesville in twenty-four hours. However Fletchley seemed eager to give it to him, so Tom followed him into the bank.

When they entered the deserted bank Fletchley's demeanour changed. He appeared to be agitated.

'I've called you in, Mr Benson, because I want a word with you.' He looked round as though fearful of being overheard.

'What about?' demanded Tom.

'You are the person who took the gold to Mexico?'

'Yes.'

'I've got some information about the gold.' Fletchley whispered the remark so that Tom almost didn't hear it.

However, the reason for Fletchley's secrecy became apparent when the bank manager came in from the back room. Even in the pale light Tom could see that Fletchley's face changed colour. Its normal healthy colour disappeared and it turned pale.

'Come inside, Fletchley, I want to see you,' ordered the manager. He gave Tom a curt nod of recognition before leading Fletchley into the back room.

Tom stepped outside the bank. He stood outside for several minutes waiting for Fletchley to come out.

When he hadn't appeared after a quarter of an hour, Tom began to weigh up his options. In reality he only had two. One was to keep on waiting until eventually Fletchley would appear. The other was to give up waiting and call in the bank tomorrow morning.

His dilemma was solved when he saw a horse riding away from the back of the bank. He recognized Fletchley as its rider. And he was riding as if at least half of the devils in hell were after him.

Since he didn't have a horse, there was nothing that Tom could do. He began to make his way back to the saloon.

It was a pleasant cool evening after the usual heat of the day. He passed a coffee shop and decided to go inside for a drink. He ordered a cup of coffee and chose a window seat so that he could watch the passers-by. Many of them were women dressed in pretty frocks who were out for an evening stroll. It was a peaceful scene. It was the sort of scene that made a person glad to be alive. That is if you didn't have several unanswered questions churning round in your mind.

He was so engrossed in his thoughts that he almost didn't catch the remark which was uttered by one particularly attractive young lady.

'I assume there's no one sitting here.'

Tom glanced up. He gave her a welcoming smile.

'It's all yours, Emily. In fact I was keeping it for you.'

'Liar,' she said, taking her seat.

When she had ordered her coffee, she said, 'Have you any Irish blood somewhere in your veins?'

'My grandmother was Irish.'

'That accounts for the blarney. Tell me, what have you been doing today?' She sipped her coffee.

'I've been in jail.'

'Visiting?'

'No, as a prisoner.'

A frown appeared on her forehead. 'What had you done?'

'According to the sheriff I started a fracas.' He described the incident.

'You shouldn't have lashed out.'

'I know. Sometimes I do things on impulse.'

'How's your head now?'

'The headache's gone. Talking to you has cleared it.'

'Are you sure you don't have half-a-dozen Irish relatives?'

'Anyhow I've solved the problem of who stole the gold.'

'You have?' She exclaimed with excitement. In fact a couple at the nearby table glanced at her.

Tom leaned forward so that she was forced to do the same. He caught a breath of her perfume. It was a long time since he had sat at a table with an attractive young lady who was wearing such a pleasant perfume. She stared at him with eager eyes.

'It's the bank manager.'

'No!' she gasped.

Again her reaction was too loud and the couple looked at her with interest.

'Come on. We'll walk,' said Tom.

Outside they began to stroll like some of the other couples who were taking the evening air.

'How did you work it out?' demanded Emily.

Tom told her about his first visit to the bank. Then about the second time when Fletchley wanted to tell him something, but was warned off by the bank manager.

'Yes, it makes sense,' said a thoughtful Emily. 'That bank manager would be in the best position to steal the money.'

He told her about his visit to the bank before he had set out with the gold. He explained that he had suggested that the army should collect the gold from the bank, but the bank manger had insisted that his men would deliver it.

'Only they didn't deliver the gold, they delivered building bricks instead,' she exclaimed.

'Exactly.'

'You've done well, Sherlock.'

'Who's he?'

'He's in some novels by an English writer. He's a brilliant detective.'

'I wouldn't say I've cracked the case yet. We still don't know where the gold is. Until I find it, I can't clear my name. People will think that somehow I'm involved in stealing the gold.'

'I don't believe you're involved. I've got complete faith in you.'

'Yes, but you're one among a thousand.'

'But I'm the important one.' Her voice seemed to have taken on a husky note. She stood on her toes and kissed him.

'That makes up for all the other nine hundred and ninety-nine,' he said, putting his arms around her and kissing her in response.

CHAPTER 6

The following morning Tom rose early. He had a busy day ahead of him.

His first call was the livery stable. The person in charge was a balding middle-aged man who was reading a newspaper in a wooden cabin by the gate.

'What can I do for you?' he demanded, as Tom stood waiting for him to look up.

'I want a horse,' said Tom.

The custodian of the livery stable put his paper to one side.

'I haven't got much selection,' he said.

'What have you got?'

'I've only got three horses. If you'll come this way, I'll show you.'

There were three horses in the small corral. Tom immediately rejected two of them since they were too small. The third held his interest.

'How old is the stallion?'

'Two years old. The person who owned him died. He was sold off with the house and the belongings.'

The horse had come over to Tom as if sensing his interest. Tom vaulted the fence. He examined its teeth and legs and ran his hand over its black coat.

'How much do you want for him?'

'Thirty dollars.'

'I'll take him.'

The other was surprised, having expected Tom to haggle.

'You can have the saddle and bridle for another ten.'

'I'll take them as well.'

Ten minutes later Tom was riding Collier down the Main Street. He was searching for a particular shop. He found it and drew up.

Having tied up the horse he stepped inside.

'How can I help you?'

The voice came from a young man, whose

name was Naylor, who stood behind the counter.

'I want a gun. A Colt.'

Naylor turned to the shelf behind him on which there was a wide array of guns. He selected five Colts and placed them on the counter. They varied from the basic Colt to inlaid mother-of-pearl ones. Tom chose one of the latter.

'It's a nice gun,' said Naylor.

'I want to test it.'

'If you'll come through the shop, you can try it out in the back.'

He led Tom out to the back where there was a washing line. On it was hung several cans. Their dents indicated that they had been used for target practice.

Tom thumbed in the bullets that Naylor had given him. He took up his position about thirty yards from the tins.

'You can go closer if you want to,' suggested Naylor.

'I'm all right here,' said Tom.

To prove his point he fired off six shots in

rapid succession. He hit a tin with every one.

'Hey! That's great shooting,' said Naylor, enthusiastically.

Tom purchased the gun and a belt and a supply of bullets. He had one more call to make.

He took the road out of town. When he had entered the town with Emily he had noticed a signpost pointing to a track leading off the road. The signpost said 'Bar T Ranch'. Tom headed towards it.

The ranch was further out of town than he had assumed. In fact it was probably about four miles outside and stood on its own in a wide expanse of short grass. Here and there cattle grazed. They looked up as Tom passed them, as if expecting to recognize him.

The ranch was a typical low wooden building with several other buildings adjoining. It was much the same as his brother's ranch in Dryden, but this one was bigger. Tom guessed that from the time he had come through the main gate to his arrival at the ranch it would be several hundred acres.

He was idly calculating the size of the ranch when he rode up to the corral. Half a dozen cowboys were there. They were watching the efforts of another cowboy to break a horse. Judging from their laughter he wasn't being too successful.

They turned round as Tom approached. He recognized one of them since he had a shock of ginger hair.

'I'm looking for a guy who hit me on the head yesterday in the Lucky Strike Saloon.'

Their laughter had died down at his approach. Now their faces changed too. There were distinct signs of apprehension on them.

'I'm waiting for one of you to own up.'

It didn't take Tom long to work out which cowboy it was since a couple of them glanced at a short, weedy cowboy. His expression, too, which was more apprehensive than the others, gave him away.

'So it was you.' Tom stood in front of him.

'I'm sorry, mister. It was a reaction. I didn't

mean to harm you.' His name was Tillson.

'It put me in jail for a few hours. It gave me a thick head. You could have killed me.'

'I'm sorry. I wasn't thinking.'

Tom was standing in front of him about twenty yards away. Suddenly the panic which had been on Tillson's face changed to terror as he realized the significance of the distance. It was the standard distance that gunslingers adopted in a shoot-out.

'I'm not a gunslinger, mister. Honest.'

Tom slowly drew his gun.

'Don't shoot me. Please,' he wailed.

Tom's reply was to aim between his feet. The bullet hit the ground an inch in front of Tillson's foot. He jumped back in terror. Tom repeated the next four bullets. Each time Tillson jumped backwards. Tom's last bullet again kicked up the dust an inch from Tillson's foot. The cowboy's retreat took him against the water butt. He was off balance and although he tried to keep to his feet he wasn't successful. He fell backwards into the water butt.

His plight was greeted with a roar of laughter from the watchers. Tom silently re-mounted his horse. Tillson was still struggling and spluttering in the water.

As Tom rode away from the ranch he could still hear their laughter. In fact he was about a couple of hundred yards away and he could still hear it. At that moment though there came a different sound. It was the sharp report of a bullet. It missed his head by the merest fraction.

Tom's reaction was instinctive. He crouched low in the saddle and dug his heels into Collier. The horse needed no second bidding.

'Someone shot at you?' Emily's voice rose with concern.

It was later in the day and Tom and Emily were seated in the coffee shop.

'Maybe he didn't like the way my hair was parted and tried to part it on the other side.'

'It's not funny, Tom. You could have been killed.'

'I've been shot at before. And I'm still here.' He put his hand over hers on the table.

'Yes, but that was in the line of duty. There was no need for you to go to the Bar T Ranch.'

'There was no way that I was going to let Tillson get off scot-free for almost killing me. I had to teach him a lesson.'

'I don't see why. Anyhow, promise me you won't go there again.'

'Don't you see, you're missing the point. Why did somebody shoot at me?'

'Because you've upset the cowboys by getting even with Tillson.'

'That's where you're wrong. When I left them they were all standing around laughing like clowns at Tillson's plight. No, somebody shot at me because I'm being a nuisance. I'm asking too many questions. I'm getting nearer the truth about what happened to the gold.'

'Yes, I suppose you could be right.' Her brow wrinkled in thought.

'I'm positive I am.'

'So what could be the connection between the Bar T Ranch and the gold bullion, Sherlock?'

'Think about it. Assume that the gold is still in Hawkesville. Where would it be hidden?'

'You'd need a shed. A large shed to keep the wagon in. That's it–' She began to get excited. 'You'd need a shed. The sort of shed that you'd find on a ranch.'

'Exactly.' Tom sat back in his seat, pleased that she had arrived at the same conclusion he had.

While she was thinking about the implications Tom ordered two more coffees.

'The problem is, how are you going to prove it,' she said, slowly.

'Yeah, that is the problem.' Tom stirred his coffee thoughtfully.

'I've got one piece of information for you,' she offered.

'What's that?'

'The detective agency, Pinkerton, are getting involved in the case. The bank has called them in. They're sending a couple of their agents here. It said so in the *New York Times*.'

'So the big boys are getting involved. That's good news.'

'So maybe you can meet these Pinkerton agents and tell them what you've found out. Then you won't have to go out and get shot at again.'

'Don't worry about me. My grandmother always used to say that I'd got the luck of the Irish.'

When they left the coffee shop and separated, Tom made his way to the sheriff's office.

He knocked and entered. The sheriff looked up. Surprise flickered on his face.

'I thought I told you to get out of town.'

Tom sat in the visitor's seat and stretched his long legs.

'I've got news for you. I'm not getting out of town.'

The sheriff's mouth tightened in anger.

'If I say you go, you go.'

'It's not your decision any longer. The big boys are getting involved. The *New York Times* is running an article about the bullion robbery. Pinkerton's are sending two agents here. They might even have arrived already. They'll want to see me. If they find out that I'm in jail on some trumped up charge, it isn't going to look too good for you. You can probably kiss your pension goodbye.'

The sheriff's unhealthy pink complexion changed to a mottled red. His mouth opened and shut as for a moment words failed him.

'The agents will want to know what you have been doing to solve the crime,' Tom continued remorselessly. 'They'll want to know what is the connection between the Bar T Ranch and the robbery. They'll want to know what questions you have asked the bank manager about who planned the robbery. In fact I would think that not only your pension, but your job isn't too safe. If I were you I wouldn't order too many bottles of whiskey.'

Tom stood up. He gave the sheriff a cursory glance. The lawman from his expression looked in a state bordering on panic. This was a person who had put him in jail without any cause. This was a person who should never have been in a position of authority. *Well, maybe he won't be much longer,* Tom reflected as he left the office.

CHAPTER 7

At six o'clock Tom was waiting outside the bank. However, this time he wasn't standing outside. This time he was mounted on his horse.

He was waiting for Fletchley to come out from the bank. Yesterday the bank official had been going to tell him something about the gold robbery, but he had been warned off by the manager. This time Tom intended to talk to him when there was no bank manager present.

Fletchley left the bank punctually at a couple of minutes past six. He rode his horse at a gallop the same as the day before. It occurred to Tom that maybe Fletchley couldn't get away from the bank quickly enough.

Tom kept at a reasonable distance behind

his quarry. The last thing he wanted was for him to become aware that he was being followed.

They were soon riding out of the town. They were in open countryside where there were houses dotted here and there. Some of them had been freshly painted and sported neat gardens, but the house that Fletchley drew in at appeared to be rundown with an overgrown yard and a fence that needed mending.

Fletchley drew up outside and dismounted. Tom, who was some two hundred yards behind, also drew up. He waited until Fletchley had gone inside before walking his horse up to the house and tying it up to a rail.

Tom knocked on the door and it took a few moments before Fletchley answered. When he did he had the face of a worried man. He glanced up and down the street before opening the door wider for Tom to enter.

'Come into the kitchen,' said Fletchley.

He led Tom into a small kitchen. There

was no fire in the grate, only yesterday's dead ashes. There were a few dishes in the sink waiting to be washed.

'I'm on my own,' said Fletchley, by way of an explanation. 'My mother died a few months' ago.'

'I'm sorry,' said Tom.

'Would you like a cup of tea, or coffee?'

Tom, having seen the state of the dishes in the sink, found it easy to refuse. 'I believe you have some information for me,' he began.

'I've got a name which might help you with your investigation. First of all I want you to realize that I'm not doing this in order to get promotion in the bank. I'm not doing it in order to get rid of the bank manager.'

The fact that Fletchley had got this confession off his chest seemed to make his relax. He stopped kneading his fingers together.

'So the bank manager is in on the robbery?'

'That's right. There are three of them—' He was interrupted by a knock at the door.

'Excuse me.' He stood up. 'I expect it's my neighbour. She always makes my dinner and brings it over for me when I come home from work.'

He went down the passage and opened the front door. Tom didn't hear what words passed, but there was no mistaking the next sound. It was that of a shot.

Tom jumped up from his chair. He dived down the passage. He was in time to hear the sound of a horse galloping away. He caught a glimpse of a man dressed in black. Tom fired a shot after the rider but he knew that he was already too far away.

He turned his attention to the figure on the doorstep. Tom had seen many dead and dying men during his years in the army and he knew without a shadow of doubt that he wouldn't give a dime for Fletchley's chances of survival. He had been shot in the heart at close range. There was a considerable amount of blood which was as Tom would expect. The only glimmer of a consolation concerning the whole tragic business was that Fletchley was unconscious. He would probably never recover consciousness and that's how he would slip into the next world in a few minutes' time.

In fact a few moments later Flethcley confirmed Tom's diagnosis by making a gentle moan. Tom searched for his pulse. There was none.

At that moment a middle-aged woman appeared on the scene carrying a saucepan. The friendly neighbour, Tom thought, as he stood in front of the body to attempt to shield her from the sight.

'I'm afraid Mr Fletchley has been shot.'

'Is he – dead?'

'I'm afraid so. Is there somebody in your house who could fetch the sheriff?'

'There's my boy, Stephen. He's seventeen. But we haven't got a horse.'

'He can take Mr Fletchley's.' He was tempted to add, *He won't be needing him now.*

It took half an hour for the law to arrive. It didn't take the form of the sheriff, but of the deputy.

Tom had covered the body with a coat which the deputy now removed.

'Who shot him?' he demanded.

'I don't know. He answered the door to someone. The next thing I heard was the shot.'

'So you didn't see him?' The deputy scratched his head. He was as unattractive a member of humanity as the sheriff. But while the sheriff was overweight, the deputy was almost alarmingly thin. He looked as though if he were to stand in a high wind he might be in danger of snapping in half.

'No. By the time I reached the door he was riding off. The only thing I saw was that he was wearing black.'

'I see.' The deputy tapped some crooked teeth with a pencil which he had produced to take down some notes. So far he hadn't taken down anything. 'Are you a friend of the deceased?'

'No. I came here because he might have some information about the bullion robbery.'

'The bullion robbery. Ah!' His tone

brightened as he came on familiar territory. 'Did you find out anything about it?'

'No. I hadn't long arrived before there was a knock at the door.'

'So he was shot before he had time to give you any information?' The deputy had taken a giant step in deduction and looked pleased with himself.

'Is there anything else you want me for?' asked Tom.

'No, you can go. I've got to stay here until the undertaker arrives,' said the deputy, as though he could think of many other things he would prefer to be doing. As Tom untied his horse the deputy added, 'Call in the office tomorrow morning to make an official statement about what happened.'

The following morning Tom set off for the sheriff's office after eating a hearty breakfast. He reasoned that there was no hurry. Fletchley was dead and no urgent meeting was going to bring him back to life.

Tom entered the sheriff's office where the

sheriff and his deputy had obviously been discussing something which was classified as secret since they both clammed up when Tom entered. He sat in the seat reserved for visitors.

'I wouldn't sit there if I were you,' said the sheriff. To Tom's surprise the sheriff accompanied his words by drawing his gun. Tom stared at him in amazement. Then he glanced at the deputy. He, too, had drawn his gun and was pointing it at Tom.

'What's this all about?' demanded Tom, racking his brains to try to find an answer.

'We're arresting you for the murder of Henry Fletchley,' said the Sheriff.

'I'll take your gun,' said the deputy, who was standing behind Tom.

He had no choice but to hand over his gun-belt.

'Why should I want to kill him? I just went to see him to get some information.'

The deputy was examining Tom's gun. 'One bullet has been fired,' he declared, with jubilation in his voice.

88

'I fired a shot after the guy who killed him. He was riding away.'

'So you fired a shot after him.' There was massive disbelief in the sheriff's voice.

'Yes, it was just a reaction.'

'It was just a reaction. But I say that the missing bullet was the one that killed Fletchley.'

'It's not true,' yelled Tom.

'And that you went to see Fletchley, not to get information from him, but to kill him, since you are one of the gang who stole the gold bullion.' The sheriff was shouting too. But it was in triumph.

'It's a pack of lies.' Tom was aware that he was still shouting, but his anger was such that he couldn't refrain from yelling back at the stupid sheriff, who looked as pleased with himself as if he'd had the winning ticket on the Kentucky Derby. 'It all fits.' The sheriff rubbed his podgy hands together.

'It's a load of rubbish. The lady next door will back up my story.'

The deputy spoke for the first time. 'I

questioned her. She said she was bringing Mr Fletchley's dinner as usual. She didn't see any rider going off.'

'So the lady next door will support your story?' sneered the sheriff. Tom found the triumph in the sheriff's tone nauseating. 'If you're going to lock me up, it could mean that the real criminals will be getting away with the gold.'

'And who are these real criminals?'

'Fletchley was going to give me one of the names when he had to go to answer the door. That's when he got shot.'

'Isn't that convenient? You never heard the name because at that moment Fletchley answered the door and got shot.' The sheriff's disbelief in Tom's story was mounting with every statement he made.

Tom was going to tell the sheriff about the fact that he had been shot at when he had visited the Bar T Ranch, but he realized he would only be adding another incident to the ones he already couldn't prove. There was one person, though, that he could implicate.

'Fletchley said that the bank manger was involved in the robbery.'

'Did he now?' The sheriff parted his thick lips in what for him was an approximation of a smile. 'Did you hear that, Studley?'

'Yes, sir,' replied the deputy. It didn't escape Tom's notice that he, too, had a smile on his thin face.

'Well, for your information, Fletchley would say that because he would like nothing better than incriminating the bank manager. A few months' ago the position of assistant bank manager came up. Fletchley thought he was bound to get it. But the bank manager gave it to the other assistant. Since then Fletchley has hated the bank manager's guts. Just as I hate yours, Mr Clever Dick Sergeant.'

Tom realized that he was hitting his head against a brick wall by trying to argue his case with the sheriff. There was only one thing for him to do. He had to wait for his trial. Then he would have a dozen reasonable men who could listen to his statements with none of the air of disbelief that pervaded the room.

The sheriff rightly interpreted Tom's silence as a temporary victory.

'All right. Take him away.' He gave the order to his deputy.

In the married quarters in the army camp, a couple of hours later, a distraught Emily burst into the major's sitting room. Her aunt was there.

'They say they're going to hang Tom. I've been to the jail but they won't let me see him.' Emily was close to tears.

'Don't upset yourself,' said Aunt Matilda.

She realized she had said the wrong thing when Emily's voice began to get hysterical.

'You don't understand. I love him. I want to be his wife. And now they're going to hang him.'

'How can you love him? You've only met him a couple of times,' said her aunt, trying to bring some vestige of reasonableness into the conversation.

'Four times. That's long enough for me to know that I'll always love him.'

'I blame the English women writers. Like that Austen woman. You've been reading too many of her books. We should have sent you to Switzerland as I suggested, not to England. But Stanley insisted you should go to England.'

'What's this got to do with Tom being hanged?' Emily wailed.

'I'm sure they're not going to hang him. At least not without a trial,' said her aunt, positively.

'Then why are they already building the gallows?'

'I don't know. It could be for some other prisoner.'

'I called in the coffee shop and they said it was for Tom,' said Emily, stubbornly.

'They can't hang somebody without a trial. Not even in Hawkesville.' Aunt Matilda rang a small bell. When a maid appeared, Aunt Matilda ordered tea. It was a custom that Emily had brought back with her from England and Matilda had adopted it willingly.

'We'll have tea and discuss the matter like civilized human beings.' She addressed the remark to the back of Emily, who was staring out through the window with an expression of complete sadness on her face.

The tea arrived and at the same time the major came into the room.

'Ah, tea,' he said, cheerfully. 'Just what I could do with to revive me.'

His wife indulged in a piece of mime by pointing to Emily's back and shrugging her shoulders.

'What seems to have upset my favourite niece,' he said, in the same cheerful tones.

Emily swung round. 'They say they're going to hang Tom.' She intended it to be a calm statement, but the effect was spoiled when her lower lip began to tremble.

'There! There! Don't upset yourself.' The major would have liked to have put his arms around her in order to comfort her, but he was not a person who could outwardly show affection. Instead he took his tea from the tray. 'I'm sure everything will be all right.'

'Emily has seen Tom on a few occasions. They seem to have become quite close,' supplied his wife.

'Do you think that was wise?' The major addressed the remark to Emily.

'Why not? I think he had a raw deal by being cashiered from the army in the first place,' said Emily, stubbornly.

Aunt Matilda could see her husband's hackles rising at the criticism of the army. In his eyes the army could do no wrong. She stepped in quickly in order to avoid a full-blown confrontation.

'We were talking yesterday about travels for Emily.'

'Oh, yes, that's right.' The major focused on the change of topic. 'How would you like to go to Switzerland, dear?'

Emily didn't even give the matter a moment's consideration.

'I can't go anywhere while Tom is in danger of being hanged.'

'Everything is arranged,' said Aunt Matilda.

'You'll be catching the stage tomorrow morning to Dryden. Then you'll go by train to Boston. From Boston you'll sail to Europe on the SS *Carlisle*. Naomi, the maid will come with you.'

'I'm not going.' A white-faced Emily faced them.

'Oh yes you are,' said the major, in tones that he had used a thousand times before to address his men. 'You will do as we tell you until you are twenty-one. That's in two months' time. After that you will inherit your money and you can do whatever you please.'

'And you will not be allowed to go into Hawksville to see Tom Benson before you go,' added her aunt.

CHAPTER 8

Tom had been in the cell for two hours. He knew because he had a compulsion to check the time by his watch at regular intervals. Nobody had visited him. His only feelings of relief had come from rolling a cigarette and smoking. The stubs on the cell floor bore testament to how many he had smoked in the past two hours.

Not only had it been quiet inside the cell, but it had also been quiet outside. When he had been in the cell before he had never noticed how quiet it was. But now, apart from the occasional shout, mostly from some wagon driver as he passed down the main street, there was surprisingly little noise.

There was one thing different from his previous visit to the cells. On that occasion all the five cells were empty, but now he had a companion. Well, not exactly a companion since he was in the next cell. He was a Mexican who had been fast asleep since the moment Tom was shown into his cell by the deputy. Tom guessed the Mexican might have been put into the cell to sleep off a hangover.

Just when Tom was thinking about how quiet it was, some distinct noises began to be heard outside. They consisted of the sounds of hammering and sawing. In addition there were several men's raised voices.

Tom went to the barred window to try to distinguish what was going on. He could see a couple of workmen, but whatever they were working on, was beyond his eyes' range. Still, the fact that there was some activity outside at last provided him with some slight points of interest.

'What the hell do they think they are doing, disturbing me like that?' The question was in Spanish and evidently came from Tom's neighbour who had been awakened by the noises outside.

'I can't see what's going on from here.' Tom answered him in the same language.

'You speak Spanish?' asked the other prisoner with surprise.

'My wife was Mexican,' Tom replied.

The Mexican had stood up. He was a thin man with the dark skin of his race. He was in his early thirties with a small moustache and an unremarkable face except for his rather large black expressive eyes. At this moment they reflected annoyance at being woken.

'My name is Paco,' he informed Tom. 'I'm afraid I can't shake hands with you. The bars are too close together.'

'I'm Tom. I'm sorry if the noise outside disturbed you.'

Paco went to the window. He could obviously see more about the activity outside since he was in line with it.

'What's going on?' demanded Tom.

When he heard Paco's answer he wished he hadn't asked the question.

'They're building a gallows.'

There was a long pause while Tom digested the remark. The pause was only interrupted by the sound of hammering.

'Are you sure?' Tom grasped at a straw.

'Positive. I can recognize a gallows when I see it.'

'Is it for you?' Tom grasped at another straw.

'No. They're going to send me back to Mexico. I've got to stand trial there.'

'Then it's for me.'

'It does seem likely.'

'It seems likely. It seems bloody definite.' Tom's voice rose in anger.

Paco wisely waited for him to cool down. Eventually he said: 'Who did you kill?'

'Nobody. I was visiting a guy from the bank when somebody knocked at the door. The next thing I knew the guy from the bank was shot by the visitor. Now the sheriff has put the blame on me.'

'The sheriff – I don't trust him. He keeps a bottle of whiskey in his desk. He was drinking some when the deputy brought me in.'

'Why have you got to stand trial in Mexico?'

'For having several wives.'

'How many?'

'Four.'

In spite of his predicament Tom chuckled.

'So you're a bigamist?'

'Several times over. The trouble is I like women.' Paco rolled his expressive eyes.

'So do I, but I doubt whether I'll be able to get near one again.'

'There is one consolation.' Paco was again looking out through the window.

'What's that?'

'They can't hang you until tomorrow.'

'How do you know?'

'They're putting cement in the holes they've dug to hold the upright timbers. The cement won't dry for several hours. So the earliest they can hang you will be tomorrow.'

'So my life depends on how long it will take cement to dry,' Tom commented.

'That's how it seems,' said Paco, who showed signs of resuming his former position on his bed.

'I hope they won't disturb you this time,' remarked Tom.

Paco's reply was to grunt. Or maybe it was a snore, Tom reflected.

In the bank manager's office three men were smoking cigars. The cigars had been supplied by the bank manager. Two of the men, the owner of the Bar T Ranch, named Sankey, and a man dressed in black, named Plover, were drinking whiskey. The bank manager, being a teetotaller, was drinking apple juice.

The three appeared relaxed, as they would after a meeting where the business of the day had been satisfactorily concluded.

'Are there any questions?' asked the bank manager.

'I don't think so,' said Sankey. 'I'll be glad to get rid of the gold. I've been losing weight ever since it's been hidden in one of my sheds.'

'There is the question of payment,' said Plover. 'I haven't received any yet for getting rid of your employee.' He addressed the remark to the bank manager.

'Yes, it was a pity about Fletchley,' said the bank manager. He reached in a drawer and produced a large envelope. 'One hundred dollars I believe was the agreed sum.' He handed the envelope to Plover.

Plover accepted the envelope. He opened it and proceeded to count out the five dollar bills. He gave a grunt of satisfaction when he realized that the number of bills was correct.

'Where are you going to go to now?' asked Sankey, casually.

'That's my business,' snapped Plover.

'Another drink?' asked the bank manager, diplomatically, in order to avoid any friction. As he poured the drinks he asked Sankey, 'I assume you're happy with your payment?'

'Five bars of gold in exchange for hiding the stuff for a week seems a good rate of payment,' smiled the rancher.

'What about the other fly in the oint-
ment?' demanded Plover, as he sipped his
whiskey.

'He's going to be hanged tomorrow,' said
the bank manager. 'They've already started
building the gallows.'

'I took a pot shot at him when he visited
my ranch,' said Sankey. 'But I missed.'

'Yes, it will be a good day's work when we
get rid of him,' said the bank manager. 'He's
been asking too many questions.'

In fact Tom was having a sound sleep for
someone who was expecting to die in the
morning. He was sleeping so soundly that it
took Paco a couple of efforts to wake him.

It was still dark but there was a full moon
which served to light up the two cells. When
Tom realized that Paco had been trying to
rouse him, he asked, 'What is it?'

'You're the person who was cashiered
from the army for being involved in the gold
robbery, aren't you?' demanded Paco.

'You didn't wake me up to ask me that, did

104

you?' grumbled Tom.

'No, I should have realized it before, but only now it occurred to me.'

'Now that you know who I am, can I go back to sleep?'

'Don't go back to sleep,' said Paco, urgently. 'I'm going to escape in a few minutes. Do you want to come with me?'

Tom hesitated for all of one second. 'Of course I want to come with you. How are you going to get out?'

'Some of my friends are coming to get me out. There's only the deputy sheriff on duty, so there won't be any problem in overpowering him.'

Was this too good to be true? Or was fate playing one of its tricks on him which it seemed to enjoy doing?

See that guy, down there? That's Tom Benson. We've played a couple of tricks on him already. We've got him cashiered out of the army. We've got him jailed on a false murder charge. Our last piece of amusement will be when he gets hanged in the morning. In the meantime we'll have one more small sport with him. We'll get him to think that he is being rescued from jail. We'll let him build his hopes up. Then we'll dash them when he discovers that it isn't true.

Yes, that just about summed up his wretched life, Tom decided.

His thoughts were interrupted by Paco.

'Put on your jacket. They're here!'

Emily knew that her only chance of seeing Tom was to go to the jail early in the morning. She knew that she must see him one more time to find out if she could help him. There must be some way of making sure that he had a trial. Surely they couldn't hang somebody just because the sheriff said that he was guilty. Especially since the sheriff was as crooked as a corkscrew.

Emily knew that the soldiers in the camp awoke early. Reveille was an hour before dawn, so if she wanted to slip into Hawkesville she had to do so in the middle of the night. The only way she could do it was to make sure that she didn't go to sleep. She selected a novel from the bookshelf and prepared to read for a couple of hours, at least until it was safe for her to leave.

She found herself nodding off several times. She was unable to concentrate fully on the book she had chosen, *The Pickwick Papers* by the English author, Charles Dickens. Normally she would have been engrossed by the antics of Mr Pickwick and the members of the Pickwick Club, but not tonight. Her thoughts kept involuntarily turning to Tom.

When she judged the time was right, she slipped out of the living quarters and out into the parade ground. From there she made her way to the stables. There was no guard on duty there so she was able to find her horse, Sally, and saddle her. She led her towards the big gate. Here she knew she might have a problem. Would the guard let her through?

To her relief the guard on duty was a Welshman named David. She had danced with him on a couple of occasions at the camp functions.

'Where are you going, miss?' he asked with a large measure of surprise.

'I'm going for a short ride. I can't sleep. I thought a ride might make me sleepy.'

To her relief he accepted the explanation. 'Don't go far.'

'I'll only ride round the camp. Anyhow, it's a nice evening.'

So saying, she sat off at a steady pace away from the camp. When she was out of sight of the guard she kicked the horse into a gallop.

Would this be the last time that she would see Tom? She almost choked at the idea. To have to go to Switzerland and never see him again. The thought was unbearable. She'd refuse to go. Yes, that's what she would do. She'd tell her aunt that she wouldn't go and if they tried to make her she'd commit suicide. That way they couldn't make her go.

During the last few days, seeing Tom had changed her whole life. She now had something to live for. Whereas before her life had seemed drab and empty, suddenly it had become meaningful and exciting. Yes, exciting, even though most of the people thought that he was involved somehow in the bullion robbery. She knew that he wasn't a criminal. He was a fine upright man. The sort of man any woman would be proud to walk out with.

What was she thinking about? She knew with one hundred per cent certainty that she would never walk out with him. This last meeting would definitely be their last. She wondered whether the meeting would present any difficulty. She had successfully managed to come out of the camp. She had remembered to bring a good supply of money with her. The chances were that she would have to bribe whoever was guarding Tom. Well, she had come prepared to do that. The money was in a pouch tied round her waist. It was all that she had been able to lay her hands on, but the guard could have it all for one last chance to talk to Tom.

She arrived at the deserted town. She slowed the horse as she rode down Main

Street. She turned into the side street that housed the jail. To her surprise there was a wagon outside. There were two Mexicans standing by it. Emily went to swing her horse round, but one of the Mexicans grabbed the bridle.

'What are you doing here, *señorita?*' he asked in Spanish.

To his surprise she answered in the same language.

'I've come to see my lover.'

'Who may that be?'

'His name is Tom Benson. He's in the jail.'

No stage actor could have timed Tom's entrance better. At that moment he came out of the jail accompanied by Paco.

'What are you doing here?' A stunned Tom directed the question at Emily.

'I came to see you.'

'What are we going to do with her?' This time the question came from one of the Mexicans and was directed at Paco.

Paco stared at the two who were looking at each other with the distinctive kind of expression that he instantly recognized. After all, he had had four wives and at some time he had shared that kind of look with all of them.

'We can't leave you here,' Paco told Emily. 'You could tell the soldiers and it would spoil everything.'

'You're taking the gold with you,' exclaimed Emily, with sudden realization.

'If you wish, we can take you with us.'

'I've always wanted to go to Mexico,' she replied.

Tom had instantly accepted the situation. He realized that there was no way the Mexicans could leave Emily behind. Unless it was a dead Emily. He didn't know whether she had grasped that fact yet. She was a very bright young lady, but now her whole being was concentrating on him, waiting for his answer.

'Then let's go,' he said, lifting her on to the buckboard of the wagon.

CHAPTER 9

They crossed the desert and the horses were splashing through the Rio Grande just as Tom's horses had enjoyed going through the river a few days before. Emily, who had been sleeping on Tom's shoulder, opened her eyes.

'Where are we?'

'Mexico.'

'I said I've always wanted to go to Mexico.' She snuggled closer to him.

'Your dream has come true.'

'They don't hang people in Mexico do they?'

'Only if they're criminals.'

'Then you're safe then.'

'Tell me something.'

'Anything.'

'How did you turn up at the jail?'

'I wanted to see you one last time.'

'Before they hanged me?'

'No, before they sent me to Switzerland.'

'Why Switzerland?'

'So that I could be as far from you as possible. But their plan didn't succeed.'

'So I see.'

Paco was sitting on the buckboard with them. 'You'll be seeing quite a lot of Mexico now that you are here.'

'Good,' replied Emily.

'He means as prisoners,' Tom explained.

'Why as prisoners?' she queried.

'Because, as Paco will confirm, the person who will now have possession of the gold will wish to keep its whereabouts a secret. The last thing he would want is for us to go wandering about in Mexico telling the authorities where the gold is.'

'That sums it up,' said Paco.

'I don't think it's a problem. As long as we're together they can do what they like with the gold,' said Emily, stubbornly.

'Are we allowed to know the name of the guy in charge?' asked Tom.

'I don't see why not. It's no secret. Any-how you'll be meeting him in a couple of hours. His name is Luis.'

'Where does he live?' demanded Emily.

'You ask too many questions,' said Paco, reproachfully.

'He lives up in the mountains,' said Tom. 'He's an outlaw. I remember hearing about him when I lived in San Caldiz.'

Having crossed the river the wagon didn't follow the usual trail that led into San Caldiz. Instead it struck out across some uncultivated land where the only signs of plant life were the occasional cactus. The ride had become more bumpy and Emily was forced to cling more closely to Tom. She smiled at him.

'I wonder what Aunt Matilda and Uncle Stanley would say if they could see me now.'

'I don't suppose we'll ever know,' Tom replied.

'I was supposed to be catching the stage to Dryden this morning. Then going by train to Boston.'

'You'll miss the easy life,' suggested Tom.

'I don't care. I can rough it if needs be.'

'You always had a servant?' demanded Paco.

'Yes – well, sort of.'

'Then you'll definitely find it different up in the camp.'

They arrived at some low foothills that obviously led up into the high mountains. Tom was surprised to see a number of Mexicans waiting for them. The wagon stopped and Paco jumped down. Tom and Emily did the same.

At the word of command from Paco the Mexicans began to unload the gold bars. Tom and Emily took the opportunity to stretch their legs.

Each of the Mexicans picked up five bars. They tied them together in the form of a cradle. They then tied the cradle round their necks and round their waist so that the bars hung securely behind them.

'I'm hungry,' said Emily.

'We'll have something to eat when they've

taken all the gold,' said Paco.

Tom and Emily sat on the ground while they watched the rest of the gold being unloaded.

'To think that that is the stuff that all the fuss is about,' said Emily.

Paco joined them.

'How much do you think it's all worth?' he asked.

'In American dollars one brick must be worth, say, a thousand dollars.' He picked up a brick that was on the back of the cart and held it in his hand. 'So if this is worth a thousand dollars then there must be a hundred thousand dollars' worth in those cases. Less the five thousand dollars that the owner of the ranch kept for himself, for hiding the wagon with the gold in it.'

'It's still a lot of money,' said Emily. 'What does Luis think he's going to do with it all?'

'You ask too many questions,' said Paco.

The last of the line of Mexicans had finished tying on his harness. They were waiting for a signal from Paco. He checked inside the wagon to see that none of the gold bars had been left inside. Then he jumped down from the wagon and waved to the waiting Mexicans.

It was the signal for them to go. They started off in single file along a path that led up into the mountain.

'Now for our food,' said Paco.

The two Mexicans who had been with them since they started off, released the horses from the wagon's shafts. The horses galloped away, delighted at their new-found freedom. Paco's next action took Emily by surprise. He set fire to the wagon.

Tom and Emily moved away from the wagon as the fire began to seize hold. Sparks were thrown up and the timber crackled beneath the devouring flames.

'I always like watching a fire,' said Emily. 'In England they set fire to a dummy every year called Guy Fawkes as a reminder that he almost blew up the King and Parliament.'

'But he didn't succeed?' demanded Paco.

'No. Some people say that it was a pity he didn't.'

When the fire was at full strength Paco kicked away part of the wooden structure that had worked loose. He gave it a few more kicks and succeeded in moving it a reasonable distance from the main fire.

'Dinner,' he said, opening a bag.

Emily peered inside.

'They're potatoes,' she said, with surprise.

Paco produced a bundle of thin sticks. He chose one and pushed its end into one of the potatoes. He put the potato into the dying embers of the fire. He nodded to Tom and Emily to do the same.

They found suitable potatoes and copied Paco's example.

When the potatoes were cooked and they had waited for them to cool, Tom and Emily tucked into them.

'Do you know, these are the best potatoes I've ever tasted,' said Emily. Her mouth was stained brown from the potato skins. She was as far from the picture of a well-brought-up young lady as she could be as she licked the remains of the meal from her fingers.

When they had finished their meal they set off. They followed the same track that the Mexicans carrying the gold had taken earlier.

At first the climb was gradual and it was easy for them to move slowly up the mountain. But gradually the path grew steeper and they were forced to pause at regular intervals to have a rest. At one of the stops Emily admired the view.

'How many feet up do you think we are now?' she asked Paco.

He shrugged. 'I don't know. Two thousand feet maybe.'

She looked at the mountain towering above. 'We're not going all the way up there, are we?'

'You ask too many questions,' he said, as they set off.

At one point they were walking along a

path that had a drop of several thousand feet to their left. The path was narrow and Emily hesitated before setting out on it.

'Don't look down,' Tom advised her. 'Just keep on looking ahead.'

She gave a sigh of relief when they had passed the spot.

'You did well,' said Paco. 'When it gets wet this part gets very dangerous.'

They had been climbing for about another half an hour when there was the sound of a gunshot.

'Where did that come from?' demanded Emily.

Paco's answer was to point to a ridge above them. She looked up and saw a dozen Mexicans, all armed with rifles.

'There's nothing to be afraid of,' said Paco. 'They're the welcoming committee.'

They had a few hundred yards to go before they came to the camp. It consisted of dozens of tents spread out on a wide plateau. As they entered it they saw that there were not only men but women and children in the camp. Those who were out-side the tents gazed at them curiously.

Paco led them to the centre of the camp. There sat a Mexican on an armchair. He had a commanding view of the camp since the armchair was on a raised dais. He was facing the sun that shone on the face of a man with greying hair and a large moustache.

'Welcome to Luis's camp,' he said, in Eng-lish.

'They both speak Spanish,' said Paco.

'So you both speak Spanish,' said Luis. He had ordered two chairs for his guests and Tom and Emily were seated in front of him.

'I was married to a Mexican woman. Unfortunately, she died.' stated Tom.

'I was sent to school in England. They taught French and Spanish,' replied Emily.

'Right. That's cleared that up,' stated Luis. 'The other question is, what are you doing here?'

'That's my fault,' said Paco, who had joined the conversation. 'Tom was about to be hanged so I let him come with us. He was a sergeant in the cavalry. He knows how to shoot. Maybe he could teach our soldiers a thing or two.'

'Yes, that could be an idea,' Luis, stroked his moustache thoughtfully.

'The young woman turned up at the jail just as we were loading the gold on to the wagon,' continued Paco. 'We didn't have much choice. We either had to bring her with us or cut her throat.'

'Yes, it would have been a pity to cut her throat. It's such a nice throat,' agreed Luis.

'You know, it's easy to go off people,' Emily addressed the remark to Paco.

'It's always easier to tell the truth,' said Paco, piously.

'Especially to your wives,' suggested Emily icily.

'You two can have your quarrel later,' stated Luis. 'In the meantime I've ordered a meal for you. It will be served in the women's tent.'

Ten minutes later they were sitting down to a tasty meal of rabbit stew, vegetables and tortillas.

When they had finished, Emily said: 'That was a lovely meal.'

The two women who had served it were pleased with the compliment.

When Tom and Emily returned to the open space between the tents where Luis was seated they were forced to wait until he had finished his conversation with one of the older men. Eventually he turned to Tom and Emily.

'How are you enjoying our hospitality so far?' he demanded.

'It's excellent,' said Tom.

'The meal was lovely,' agreed Emily.

'You will see that our hospitality hasn't ended yet. It's too late to arrange anything this evening, but tomorrow I will arrange a fiesta. The arrival of the gold is a perfect excuse. There will be wine, women and dance. You will find that even in this far from perfect environment, we still know how to enjoy ourselves.'

'We'll look forward to it,' stated Tom. 'There is one question I would like to ask.'

'Yes?'

'What are our sleeping arrangements going to be while we are here?'

'There are not two spare tents. The best I can offer is that you can share a tent. Of course you can have separate mattresses.'

'That will suit us,' said Emily. 'It will give me a chance to find out whether he snores before we get married.'

Both Luis and Paco grinned at her remark. Tom scowled as she led him away.

When they reached the tent, Emily asked: 'Do you want the right-hand mattress or the left?'

'It doesn't matter.' He stood in front of her. 'I don't think you realize the serious-ness of our position. You think all this is a bit of a joke. Well, it isn't. Those outlaws are killers. They will slit your throat if they think they can gain something by it. At the moment everything in the garden is rosy because they've got the gold. But things can change. Our only hope of survival is to get out of here. I don't see any chance of that at the moment but we must keep on our guard, and when we see a chance to escape, take it. Do you understand?'

'I like it when you're being masterful,' she said, giving him a brief kiss.

'Oh, what the hell!' said Tom, as he stretched out on one of the mattresses.

Loretta's skirt rose higher as she spun energetically round. Her red dress took on a darker hue as the evening sun shone on it. Her black hair, piled up and held in place by a gold-coloured comb, added to the perfect picture that her dancing figure portrayed.

A three-piece band accompanied her movements. Seated on the rostrum behind her, they kept time to the stamping of her heels and the clicking of her tambourines. Emily stared at Loretta admiringly.

'She's great, isn't she?'

Tom thought that she was quite good. But not as good as his Carlotta had been. It was funny though the way he could now think of Carlotta, dispassionately. In the past when he had thought of her it had been as if a pain had seared though his brain. When he thought of the way she had died and of how their child had died, he had felt that he could never come to terms with it without the terrible pain of loss. But now he could compare Carlotta's dancing with Loretta's and think about it quite calmly.

'I suppose so.'

Emily stared at him.

For a young girl it seemed as though sometimes she could almost read his mind. He had seen very little of her all day. They had slept late and she had waked first.

'Come on, sleepyhead, time to get up,' she had announced.

While he was shaving with a cracked mirror and an open razor that a Mexican named Alphonso had brought to him, she had left the tent to go about her own devices. He found out later that in fact she had joined the women who were washing their clothes. They went to a stream where they undressed and rubbed the garments over some rocks in order to get them clean. Although the stream was a fair distance away Tom could hear the women's laughter as they washed themselves and the clothes in the stream.

When he had finished shaving, Alphonso's wife brought him some hot tortillas and some coffee. After he had eaten he said to Alphonso: 'Tell your wife that they were the best tortillas I have ever tasted.'

'I will tell Anna. She will be delighted to hear it.'

The food was excellent, Emily was obviously enjoying herself in the company of the camp women so why did he feel that it was too good to be true? That any minute fate would step in and deliver its usual body-blow?

It did – but not until later in the day, while the fiesta was in full swing. Luis called him to the chair which Emily had dubbed his throne.

'Are you enjoying the festivities?' demanded Luis politely.

'They are excellent,' Tom confirmed.

'Good. Now I have to ask you a small favour.'

'What is it?'

'Paco mentioned that you were in the American cavalry.'

'That's right. The Eleventh Cavalry.'

'So you have quite a knowledge of horses?'

'I think so. I was in charge of fifty horses for some time.'

'Good. Now as you know I've got gold with which I can buy anything. To start with I need horses. As you saw, you and my men had to walk up the mountain. I want mountain ponies so that in future we carry supplies on them. Also, of course, they will be useful to help to protect us against any attackers.'

'How can I help?'

'I want you to go and buy the horses for me. None of my men knows anything about horses. If one of them went down to buy them they'd end up with some old nags that wouldn't last a few months.'

For a fleeting moment Tom saw it as a

possible chance of escape.

'Where do I get them from?'

'It's a farm just outside Limos, I will tell you how to get there.'

'What about Emily? Can she come with me?'

'Certainly not. She stays here. She's our insurance that you will come back.'

CHAPTER 10

Tom had taken leave of a tearful Emily and was on his way to the farm. Emily had clung to him for several minutes before finally letting him go.

'You will come back, won't you?' she wailed.

'Of course I will.' He brushed away a tear from her eye.

'But there's nothing stopping you from riding off. You could go anywhere. You could be free.'

'I'll pretend I didn't hear that.'

'There's nothing to stop you going away,' she persisted.

'Oh, yes there is.'

He took her in his arms and kissed her hard.

When they parted he said: 'Now do you

think I'll ride off and leave you here?'

She forced a smile: 'No, I suppose not.'

'Right. Then get all those stupid thoughts out of your mind. Enjoy yourself in the company of the other women. I should be back in a couple of days.'

He and Paco set off down the mountain path. When they came to the bend which would take them out of sight of the camp, Tom turned. Emily was standing on a rock so that she would have a good view of them before they disappeared from her sight. She waved with both hands.

'She is a lovely lady,' Paco informed him. 'If I had a woman like that who loved me the way she loves you, maybe I would have settled for just one wife.'

'If I believed that, I'd believe anything,' Tom replied.

'Yes, I suppose I'm a bigamist at heart,' Paco agreed.

'What about you being wanted for trial? If we go to Limos, won't the police put you in jail?'

'Limos has its own police and its own mayor. It's run by a villain named Zapote. He's friendly with Luis.'

'So you're not wanted for bigamy in Limos. Only in San Caldiz,' Tom concluded.

'That's right.'

They descended the mountain in silence. Tom noticed that the path they were using was more gradual than the one they had used from San Caldiz. In fact they reached Limos in a couple of hours without having to negotiate any tricky narrow paths and especially any with a large drop on the side if a person happened to lose his footing.

'This path is an improvement on the one from San Caldiz,' observed Tom.

'This is the way Luis will take his horses when we have bought them,' explained Paco.

When they reached the plain Paco struck off to the left, although Limos could be seen in the distance on the right.

'We're not going into town,' stated Tom.

'When we have bought the horses, then we

will go into town. We will spend the night there. I am friendly with a *señorita*. I haven't seen her for some time.'

'I should have guessed,' said Tom.

They had about another mile to walk before they reached the farm. As they approached it Tom could see that there were several dozen horses in a paddock.

A thick-set, middle-aged Mexican came out to greet them.

'What can I do for you?' he demanded.

Paco explained who they were and why they had come.

'Luis wants horses?' There was surprise in the farmer's voice, whom Paco had introduced as Diego.

'Yes. And of course he can pay for them now, since he's come into money.'

Diego roared with laughter. 'Yes, I've heard that he's come into a fortune.'

'My friend here was a captain in the American cavalry,' stated Paco. 'He's an expert on horses. He'll choose thirty of yours.'

Diego studied Tom before replying.

'I think it would be a good idea if you had a drink in the first place. You both look as though you could do with one.'

Diego let them into the house. Like most Mexican houses it was cool inside.

'I'll have to get the drinks myself,' stated Diego. 'My wife is at the market in Limos.' He disappeared into the kitchen.

'Do you think you'll be able to find thirty horses?' demanded Paco.

'I had a quick look at them. They seem in good condition, although I'll have to take a closer look before I can decide properly.'

Diego came back with two glasses. 'I'm afraid I haven't got whiskey,' he said. 'Only tequila.'

'That's fine by me,' said Paco.

Tom accepted the glass although tequila wasn't his favourite drink. In fact he thought the drink was rather sweet, but he was thirsty and so downed it quickly.

'Would you like another one?' demanded Diego.

'No, thanks,' replied Tom. 'I'll have a look

at the horses in a minute or two. How many have you got?'

'Sixty,' replied Diego. 'Although some of them are only a few months' old and you wouldn't be interested in them.'

'No, I'd want them at least a year old.'

'I think you'll find there'll be enough for you. Do you want mares or stallions?'

'Either, as long as they're in good condition.'

'Oh, they're all in good condition. We get a horse doctor to examine them regularly.'

'Thatch good,' replied Tom. Why was he slurring his words? He'd only had one drink, yet he was sounding as if he'd had half a dozen. Maybe if they went out into the fresh air it would clear his head. 'Can I shee them now?' he asked.

He was still slurring his words. Yes, he'd better go outside. He stood up. As he did so the room began to move. At first it tilted to one side. Then it tilted alarmingly to the other side. In fact it tilted so much that he was forced to hang on to the table to keep his balance.

Diego, too, had stood up. He was standing in front of Tom. The strange thing was that Diego's face was growing. It was expanding like a balloon. In fact Diego's smile was so big that it was a wonder that it didn't touch the walls.

Then the truth hit Tom with the force of a thunderbolt.

'You've drugged me.'

This time he didn't slur the words. Instead he collapsed to the floor on his face.

Paco didn't visit his woman in Limos as he had planned. Instead, a few minutes after Tom had collapsed in a drugged heap, he had been faced with a situation to which there was no alternative.

As soon as Paco realized what was happening to Tom he had reached for his only weapon, his knife. But Diego was quicker. He was already covering him with his revolver.

'You won't need that,' he said, taking his knife from him. 'All you have to do is to take a message.'

If he was going to carry a message, then, Paco reasoned, Diego wasn't going to shoot him. His spirits rose slightly.

'What message?'

'I want you to tell Luis that if he wants to see his horse-buyer alive he'll have to pay for the privilege.'

'How much?'

'Two gold bars.'

'But that's–' Paco struggled to calculate how much that would be worth, but without success.

'Yes, I know. A lot of money. But that's the condition. Otherwise the *gringo* will have his throat cut from ear to ear.'

So Paco set off back up the trail. He was not a happy Mexican. His plans had been scuppered by Diego. His girlfriend, Esmeralda, would have provided him with many of the essentials of life which he had missed up in the mountain camp. She was young and nubile. She kept coming back for more. After their lovemaking he wouldn't have had the strength left to climb the path energetically the way he was doing now.

He had to face facts. He doubted whether he would see her in the near future. If so it only left him with one alternative. He would have to take one of the girls in the camp to bed. Of course as a second choice it wasn't too bad. The advantage of being in the camp was, for some reason that Paco had never been able to fathom, that there were more women than men. At least two of the young women were very attractive. Yes, very attractive indeed.

Of course he would have to promise to marry one of them. That would be the price he would have to pay to get her to come to bed. But since the women didn't know about his past history there shouldn't be any difficulty if he had to make that promise. Yes, the more he thought about it, the alternative to Esmeralda could be of some advantage to him. Presumably he would be up in the camp for some time. He could even marry one of the two women. It would mean that she would cook for him as well as looking after his other needs.

Of course there was the question of what was going to happen to Tom. Well, that was out of his hands. That was a decision that Luis would have to take. He began to hurry, since he wanted to make sure that he arrived in the camp before it became dark.

In fact the camp was almost in complete darkness when he arrived. There were just a few lanterns giving light at strategic places. One of these was situated near Luis's chair and lit up its occupant's face.

'Well?' demanded Luis as Paco approached. 'Why are you on your own?'

'Things didn't work out as planned–' Paco began.

'So I see. Otherwise you'd have brought Benson with you. Where is he?'

'Diego kidnapped him. First of all he drugged him by putting opium in his tequila.'

'Why would Diego want to kidnap Benson?' demanded a puzzled Luis.

'He wants you to pay him two gold bars to

get him released.'

'What?' Luis roared. Then realizing that he might have awakened some of the camp he lowered his voice. 'Who does Diego think he is, trying to get my gold like this?'

'I'm just passing on the message,' pleaded Paco.

'Well you can go back down and pass on my message,' stated Luis. 'No way am I going to give two gold bars to get Benson released.'

'Diego said that if you didn't pay he'd slit Benson's throat from ear to ear.'

'Let him go ahead and do it,' snapped Luis. 'I'll get my horses some other way.'

The following morning Paco stayed in his tent. He didn't join the others for breakfast.

He had two reasons for trying to stay in hiding. In the first place he hoped that Luis, who was a late riser, had regretted his decision not to send the two bars of gold for Tom's release. The second reason was that he wanted to keep out of Emily's way. He knew that once she knew about Tom's predicament she would stop at nothing to get Luis to pay Diego with the gold.

He was right. Sometime in the morning Emily learned about Luis's refusal to hand over the gold. There was no doubt that she was upset by Luis's decision. She was so upset that she was screaming at him as he sat in his chair.

'It's only two bars of gold, for God's sake! You'll still have ninety-eight left.'

'Ninety-three,' Luis corrected her. 'Somebody took five bars before I received it.'

'All right. Ninety-three. You're still as rich as Croesus. What are two bars to you?'

'It's my gold and I intend keeping it,' shouted Luis, stubbornly.

Emily turned to the Mexicans who had gathered around to listen to the argument.

'Don't you think he should pay two bars to get Tom's release?'

When it came to having to make a decision, many of them turned away, some with shame-faced expressions.

'All right. So none of you have got any fight in you,' Emily stormed. 'But I'm prepared to fight for the man I love.' She turned to Paco. 'Take me down to see this Diego. I've got a few hundred dollars – American dollars. It might not be worth as much as two bars of gold, but it might be enough to make Diego release Tom.'

Paco turned to Luis for guidance. Luis shrugged his shoulders. Paco rightly translated it into, 'You can do what you like.'

'I'll be ready after I've eaten,' said Paco.

In Diego's house Tom was slowly recovering consciousness. He opened his eyes to the realization that he was tied to a chair. The reason for his position gradually seeped into his mind.

He had been drugged. Diego had drugged him. He had thought the tequila was too sweet and he had been right. It had contained diluted opium.

Once the reason for his position had been established, Tom had to consider two questions. The major one was what was he going to do next? The secondary one was what did Diego think he was going to gain by drugging him?

Tom glanced around. He was in the room where Diego had brought him and Paco when they had hoped to negotiate the deal about buying the horses. He was tied firmly to the chair. That fact only took Tom a couple of seconds to establish. The only slight advantage he had at the moment was that Diego wasn't in sight. Possibly he was outside tending to his horses. But it gave Tom a chance to think about some method of escape. The only trouble was, at the moment he couldn't think of one.

He glanced around the room. There was a lack of furniture. There was just a table and three chairs round it. Presumably the chair to which he was tied would complete the number of chairs which would be used for meals.

Tom stared at the table. It was an ordinary bare table, but it did have one item which might be of interest. It had a drawer. A drawer with a distinctive knob. It was the sort of knob which, if he could reach it, he might be able to use to open the drawer.

His first problem was how to reach the drawer. He tried moving the chair. To his relief there were no mats on the floor – it was just a plain wooden floor. This meant that he was able to inch his way towards the drawer.

His progress was slow. At any moment he expected Diego to enter the room and spot that he had moved from his original position to one near to the table. But to his relief there was no sign of the Mexican.

He reached the table. Next was another difficult manoeuvre. Could he open the drawer with his teeth?

He bent over the table, seized the drawer with his teeth and gave it a tug. To his relief it moved a few inches. Also to his inexpressible relief he glimpsed what he had hoped to see inside it – a knife.

For the next few minutes he pulled the

drawer open, inch by inch. As more of the knife was revealed Tom's hopes soared.

Diego had made one mistake when he had tied Tom. He had assumed that since he was drugged it didn't matter too much how he tied him. As a result he had tied Tom with his hands in front of him. If he had tied Tom with his hands behind him Tom would never have been able to try to embark on his next movement to try to escape. He put his hands into the drawer.

If he had thought that opening the drawer with his teeth was a tricky manoeuvre, his next step in his attempt to escape was even harder. He had to grasp the knife between his fingers. Then turn it upright so that the blade was at right-angles to the bottom of the drawer. Then he had to try to saw through the cords.

It took him several attempts before he could grasp the knife between his fingers. The sweat was standing on his brow as he failed after the first few attempts. In fact he was beginning to doubt that he would be able to grasp the knife successfully, when suddenly he succeeded! He was holding the knife between his fingers and sawing through the cords.

A few minutes' later his hands were free. He hastily sawed through the cords binding his legs and stood up. He was walking round the room to try to restore his circulation when suddenly the door was flung open. Diego stood there. The bad news was he was holding a revolver in his hand.

'Put the knife on the table,' Diego commanded.

He must have seen me through the window, Tom concluded, as he obeyed the command.

In order to make it as difficult as possible for Diego to get hold of the knife, Tom placed it as far away from him as he could. Diego stretched over to grasp the knife. For a split second he wasn't covering Tom with the gun. Tom acted swiftly. He tipped the table over. It landed on its side with a crash. Diego jumped back to try to avoid being knocked over by it. Even so he was forced to hold on to the table. The result was that Diego dropped his gun.

Both the knife and the gun were out of Tom's reach, but Diego was within his range. He hit him with a well-timed right to the side of the face that could have put many men out of action for at least a few seconds. But Diego wasn't going to be an easy opponent to beat. He actually grinned as he tried to rise to his feet.

Tom dived on him. They tried to smash each other's faces as they rolled over the floor. Tom succeeded with a couple of blows but the fact that they were moving took the power out of them. Diego succeeded in landing one of his own, and Tom tasted his own blood as the punch split his lip.

In weight there was little to choose between them. Tom was taller than Diego and if they managed to fight on their feet then his height could be an advantage. Diego, on the other hand, was more stocky, but still solidly built.

Their efforts to land a telling blow took

them to the open door. After a few more in-effective attempts at gaining the upper hand they had rolled out into the open. The horses were in the enclosure nearby and some neighed as if encouraging one or other of the fighters.

Tom was becoming painfully aware that the form of half-wrestling, half-fighting in which they were indulging was suiting Diego. He was definitely more of a wrestler than a boxer. Evidence of this could be seen in the way he tried to crush Tom's ribs at every opportunity, and the fact that Tom was finding it difficult to breathe every time Diego succeeded in his plan.

Tom would have liked to stand up. But he knew that if he did so he would be handing the advantage to Diego. All Diego would have to do would be to grab Tom round the legs, bring him crashing down to the ground and Tom would definitely be the loser.

They were continuing their crab-like pro-gress towards the horses' enclosure.

Diego managed to land another telling

blow on the side of Tom's face. It took Tom a couple of seconds to realize that he was weakening. Maybe the effects of the drug hadn't completely worn off, or maybe the fact that he hadn't had a meal for over a day was contributing to his weakness. Whatever the reason, Diego was landing more telling punches like the last one, and his own had become merely slaps which Diego had easily parried.

The situation was becoming desperate. Tom knew that he couldn't last much longer before Diego managed to land a knock-out blow. They were now against the wooden fence that guarded the horses. In fact Tom was right up against it and Diego gave a grunt of satisfaction, thinking that Tom could go no further. He realized that he was gaining the upper hand and landing one more strike could spell the end of the contest for Tom.

Tom knew that he had one chance of escape. He took it. He stood up and vaulted over the fence. The horses were milling about and Tom was forced to avoid them. Diego gave a roar at thinking that his quarry was escaping. He, too, leapt over the fence. Tom's plan to grab one of the horses and jump up on it was thwarted when Diego dived for his legs. They both ended up on the ground. Tom realized with growing horror that hardly anything had changed. Diego was still intent on hitting him into oblivion. The only difference was that now the horses had become excited and were neighing loudly as they tried to avoid the struggling humans on the ground.

Diego was pounding at Tom's face, trying to land the final punch. Tom was evading some of them with a turn of the head, but knew that one blow on his jaw would spell the end of the contest, which was now becoming increasingly uneven. His chances of survival were lessened further when a horse's hoof landed a few inches from his face and he was forced to turn to face Diego. This presented his opponent with a ready-made target. Diego took full advantage of it and landed a piledriver of an upper cut on Tom's jaw. Tom felt that he was slipping into the world of unconsciousness.

'Hang on, Tom!' It was almost as if he could hear a voice encouraging him. He knew without a shadow of doubt that the voice was Emily's. It gave him one last glimmer of hope.

Diego, thinking that Tom was finished when he had delivered the killer blow, leaned back to wait for Tom to collapse completely. However, from some unknown depth, spurred by the voice in his mind, Tom summoned up one last attack. Whereas until that moment Diego's face had been moving, making it difficult for Tom to land a decisive strike, now Diego was staring at him. And Diego's face was within range. Tom hit him with a right hook which would have pleased his boxing instructor in the army.

The punch landed perfectly on Diego's jaw. The Mexican's eyes glazed. He slumped backwards.

Tom had no time to admire his handiwork. One of the horses which had been milling around suddenly reared. Tom watched, expecting it to come back down to earth. To his horror it did. Only it landed on Diego's face. Tom could have sworn that he heard the sound of Diego's skull cracking under the horse's weight.

CHAPTER 11

At about the same time that Tom was struggling with Diego, Emily was also struggling with a man. This one too was a Mexican.

She had been waiting for Paco to finish his meal. While she was waiting the wildest of ideas occurred to her. Perhaps she could steal two gold bars. After all the money didn't belong to Luis – it actually belonged to the bank, so she wouldn't really be stealing. Luis was the one who was the thief in the eyes of the law.

She knew that the gold bars were being kept in a wooden shed on the edge of the camp. Of course it would be locked, and it would be guarded, but maybe she could persuade the guard at least to let her look at the bars. Yes, it might be worth a try. She could even try to influence him with her feminine wiles. If it came to the crunch she would even be willing to surrender her body to him if it meant that she could get Tom's release.

She strolled over to the shed. As she had expected there was a guard on duty. He watched her approach with interest. When she was getting nearer she swung her hips in an impression of the women of the night that she had seen in England. The guard was even more interested.

Round one to her, she thought. Now came the difficult part.

'My name is Emily,' she said.

'I know. I've heard about you. My name is Samson.'

'Are you as strong as the man in the Bible?'

Samson smiled. He bent his arm so that his muscle showed. 'Feel that.'

She did as he requested. Her movement had brought her close to Samson. In fact her body was almost touching his. She kept her eyes fixed on his face.

Now was his chance. He willingly accepted the invitation. He kissed her savagely.

It meant nothing more to her than a stage kiss. In England she had been in several plays, and had been in considerable demand as an actress. If she had stayed in England she could have joined one of the touring companies that were travelling round the country putting on the plays of Shakespeare, Sheridan or Goldsmith.

Samson showed every sign of wanting to continue with his kisses, so she went ahead with her plan.

'Let's go inside. It's too public out here.'

He hesitated. He knew that if Luis ever found out then his life wouldn't be worth a peseta. But what this blonde girl was offering him was surely worth more than his life. To have some time alone with her would be something beyond his wildest dreams. Anyhow Luis would never know. He was too busy with one of his own paramours at this moment.

Samson quickly unlocked the door and

they stepped inside. There was one small window in the shed. It gave sufficient light to see the gold bars that were stacked on a couple of shelves.

They looked quite innocent sitting on the shelves, but they had already been responsible for Tom almost being hanged, for Tom being held at ransom for a couple of them, for her being raped in exchange for them. Oh, no! Her mind recoiled at the thought.

Samson had pressed her against the wall. She was struggling to stay on her feet since his obvious intention was to pull her down on to the floor. Samson was hurting her as he pressed against her. 'Don't faint, Em!' she told herself over and over again. She knew that if she did, then she would be completely at his mercy.

Samson was too strong for her. He succeeded in pulling her down to the ground. He lay on top of her and tugged at her dress. He grunted as the material refused to rip. It was made of good quality cloth that she had bought while in London.

Samson changed his tactics. He fumbled under the dress. She desperately tried to keep his hand from reaching its goal. But once again he proved too strong for her. She shrieked as his hand touched her bare flesh.

Samson gave a grin of satisfaction. They were spreadeagled on the floor so that there was no chance of her getting away from him. He knew that he had her at his mercy.

Although Emily realized this too it didn't stop her from struggling. She was still holding on to Samson's hand which was fumbling between her legs. His face was touching hers. He had kept this position after she had tried to gouge his eyes. It had proved to be an ineffective method of trying to stop him since they were continually moving and she missed his eyes by a considerable margin. All she had succeeded in doing was scratching his face.

He had given a roar of frustration at her attempt to gouge his eyes. He had raised his fist with the obvious intention of giving her a stunning blow. In fact his fist stayed poised for several seconds. She closed her eyes waiting for the blow to come. But it never arrived.

When she opened her eyes she could see that Samson had a bigger grin on his face than before. It took her a few moments to realize its implication. When she did she spat at his face. Samson ignored it and continued scrabbling with his hands beneath her petticoat.

She knew now why he hadn't knocked her unconscious when he had had the chance. It was because he was getting far more satisfaction while she was conscious and struggling the way she was. She had realized something else. The more she was struggling, the more it increased Samson's desire. And the more satisfaction he was getting from the assault.

He was lying on top of her and trying to force her legs apart. She was keeping them together with every ounce of strength in her being. Why didn't somebody come past the shed? The door was hanging unlocked.

Surely somebody would see it and come inside to find out what was happening.

The main thing in Samson's favour was that the shed was some distance away from the camp. She knew that she should scream. That would surely bring somebody. But she knew with one hundred per cent certainty that if she did Samson would deliver the knock-out blow he had threatened before. She would have no resistance to his desire. Before somebody would arrive she would be completely at his mercy.

He was succeeding in forcing her legs apart. He grunted with the effort. He slipped off his trousers. She knew that she was only a few seconds away from being raped. There was still one glimmer of hope though. When he had kicked off his trousers Samson had momentarily partly rolled off her. With a huge effort she managed to slide from under him. She staggered to her feet. Samson, who hadn't completely taken off his trousers, grabbed one of her legs as he saw that his intended victim might yet escape his clutches.

Emily struggled to keep her balance. She grabbed the edge of one of the shelves in an effort to prevent Samson from pulling her back down to the floor. Her fingers touched one of the gold bars. She didn't hesitate. She grabbed it. As Samson rose to continue their struggle he was met by a sharp blow on the head from the gold bar. The blow was hard enough to make him slide to the floor and howl with pain. He was about to try and rise when they both heard another sound. It was an eerie sound which at one time in the past had echoed in many parts of Texas and North Mexico. It was the war cry of the Apache Indians.

Emily watched through the narrow slit in the partly open door as the Apaches rode into the camp. The warriors were all stripped to the waist and their faces were painted with yellow and black stripes. They presented a terrifying sight.

They were whooping as they fired at the

Mexicans. Emily couldn't see how many there were because her view was restricted. The last thing she wanted was to open the door fully in case it attracted attention to their whereabouts.

Some of the Mexicans were firing back at the riders as they circled the camp. But the sounds of the shots were sporadic. Emily guessed that most of the Mexicans had been completely taken by surprise and hadn't had time to get their guns.

What was going to happen to her? The question struck her like a hammer blow. She had escaped from the clutches of Samson, but what if an Apache decided to look into the cabin? There was no possibility of Samson shooting it out with the Apaches. He was lying on the floor having been rendered unconscious by her blow with the gold bar. He would take no further interest in whatever was going to happen to them.

The gold bars! That was why the Apaches had attacked the camp. It was strange that she hadn't realized it before. Somehow or other they must have found out about the gold. As a result they had decided to attack the camp and seize the gold for themselves.

If that was so, it put her in an even more precarious position than she had thought. If they had come for the gold then it was as sure as God made little green apples that they weren't going away without it. Which meant that at some stage an Apache warrior was going to open the door of the cabin and discover the two inhabitants and the gold. Although it was the hottest part of the day she grew ice cold at the thought.

Was there any chance of her escaping from the hut? At the moment the Apaches were busy quelling any resistance in the main part of the camp. Could she take a chance and make a dash for the mountain path? She rejected the idea as soon as it occurred to her. At least one of the Apaches would be bound to spot her since the path was a couple of hundred yards away. No, there was no way that she could escape.

Among the sporadic rifle fire there were

other sounds – of women screaming. She shuddered as she listened to them. She guessed they were being subjected to the same horrible physical assault that she had just escaped from. Some of them were probably her friends. Even in the short time she had been in the camp she had made a few friends among the younger women. Maybe some of the screams she was hearing came from them. She put her hands over her ears to try to blot them out.

Why hadn't Luis been prepared for such an attack? He should have known that his gold would be a target for outlaws or renegades. The least he should have done should have been to see that the men in the camp had adequate guns. The fact that the shooting had now died down proved that they hadn't been sufficiently armed. True, he had sent Tom to buy some horses, but it would have been more important for him to have bought guns.

Tom! Where was he now? When he returned to the camp he would be horrified at what he would find. He was used to seeing corpses in his profession as a soldier, but he would never expect to see the whole camp wiped out – she was sure that was what had happened in the past hour or so. At this moment she didn't know whether the Apaches had spared the women. If they had then it was her only faint chance of survival.

At that moment the thing that she had dreaded came to pass – an Apache rode up to the hut. He dismounted and flung open the door. He gave a whoop of joy at seeing the gold. At seeing Emily crouching in the corner he gave another whoop.

The Apache had his gun at the ready. He shot Samson at point-blank range. He grabbed Emily by the arm and pulled her out of the hut. He was incredibly strong. He tucked her under his arm as though she were a doll. He jumped up on his horse.

'Geronimo!' he cried as he rode away.

Tom dragged the body of Diego away from

the panicking horses. He felt no pity. The Mexican had drugged him and would presumably have killed him if he had not been given the gold. The only concession to respect for the dead was that he carried the body into the house. He knew that if he left the corpse for any length of time in the open then vultures would soon find it.

In the house he found his gun-belt and gun. Then he returned back to the horses' compound. He didn't intend walking back up to the camp. He wanted a horse which the dead Diego would have provided if he hadn't been so greedy.

Tom chose a horse. It was smaller than the standard cavalry horses but he guessed that it would probably be more useful on the mountain paths. He thought for a moment and picked a second horse, thinking of Emily and their escape. He found saddles and bridles in a separate shed and was soon on his way riding back up the path he and Paco had walked down the previous day, leading the spare horse behind him.

As he rode along he thought of Emily. There was no doubt she was quite a girl. Well, not exactly a girl, but every inch a woman as he could testify by the few times he had held her in his arms. She was the sort of woman a man could easily imagine himself spending the rest of his life with. She was attractive, she was loyal, she had a nice sense of humour. Yes, she was everything a man could wish for in a wife.

Why was he contemplating marriage? He had sworn when Carlotta had died that he would never, under any circumstances, marry again. Now here he was thinking about Emily as a possible future bride.

There were a couple more urgent problems to be overcome first. They had to get away from Luis's camp. It wasn't going to be easy. The fact that Luis had kept Emily in the camp while he had sent him down to see about buying the horses, proved that Luis intended keeping them there.

There was, however, one glimmer of hope in any plan for them to make their escape.

He now had a horse. Whereas previously any thoughts of escape were necessarily confined to them going down the mountain on foot, he could now get away quickly from the camp. The sturdy mountain ponies could carry the two of them to safety. He and Emily could make a break for it. If Luis sent some of his so-called soldiers to try to catch them – well, he had a gun and plenty of ammunition. If it came to a shoot-out on the mountain he'd back his skill as a marksman against any of Luis's outlaws.

Yes, the more he thought about it, the more it became a distinct possibility. Knowing Emily, the chances were she would be watching for him to arrive up the mountain path. If he could signal to her, she could come down to meet him. Then he could turn around and the two could make their escape. It would take some of Luis's men several minutes to get their horses. In that time they could be well on their way to freedom.

Of course he was assuming that Luis

wouldn't have paid the two gold bars for his release. Anyhow, that was all in the past since he was now on his way to the camp and should reach it soon.

In fact he rounded the next bend and could see the plateau where the camp stood. His heart lurched when he saw something else. The camp was no longer there. Where the tents should have been were now only empty spaces with smoke drifting idly into the air.

The camp had been burned down. He kicked the horse to move more quickly up the path while he stared in disbelief at the remains of the camp.

Who could have done such a thing? Presumably another outlaw gang who knew about the gold. The main question was, what was he going to find when he reached the plateau?

He discovered the terrible truth when he arrived at the first remains of the tents and jumped down from his horse. There were bodies outside the tents. In fact as far as he could see there were bodies outside every tent. It was easy to work out that the Apaches were responsible for the carnage – most of the corpses had been scalped.

He dashed around the tents searching for Emily. There were bodies of women lying everywhere. The Apaches hadn't been selective in choosing whom they had killed. They had killed everybody – including children.

Tom had heard of blood-baths like this when the Indians had sought revenge on the white man for the way they had been treated. But he had never thought he would experience it at first hand. And where was his beloved Emily?

He came to the seat that was normally occupied by Luis. It was empty. Maybe the Apaches had taken some prisoners. Maybe they had taken the camp chief, Luis, with them. Maybe Emily had also been one of their captives. His mind grasped at the straw as he dashed round from tent to tent.

He soon discovered his error when he

found Luis's body outside one of the tents. Like the others he too had been scalped. One of the differences between Luis's body and that of the other Mexicans was that he wasn't wearing his trousers. It didn't take a genius to work out what Luis had been doing when the Apaches arrived.

'If you're looking for the fair-haired young girl, the Apaches have taken her.' The words were spoken by a strange-looking character who had stepped out from a wooden shed. It took Tom a few seconds to realize that he was a half-caste, but not the usual Mexican–American. This one was an Apache–Mexican.

'Then she was alive!' Tom couldn't keep the excitement out of his voice.

'I saw one of the braves riding off with her. Carlos would swear it on the Bible.'

'There's no need for that,' said Tom, sharply. 'You must have come with the Apaches,' he said, in a more conciliatory tone.

'That's right, I was brought up by the Apaches.'

'Why didn't you go back with them?'

'You've seen what they did here. To the women and children. Carlos never wants anything more to do with them.'

Tom thought for a moment. 'How far is their camp?'

'A day's ride.'

A day's ride. Probably about twenty miles. For the cavalry a day's ride meant thirty miles. 'Are you willing to ride with us to the Apaches camp?'

'Who's us?'

'I'm going to fetch some soldiers. We'll be back here in two days. If you will show us where the Apache camp is I can guarantee that you will be well paid.'

Carlos hesitated. Finally he said. 'I don't want your money. It will be enough to get revenge for what the Apaches did here.'

'So you'll stay here until we come back?'

'I swear that I will stay. Carlos always keeps his word.'

Tom mounted his horse and was about to ride off when Carlos stopped him.

'I found this in the shed.'

He handed Tom a ribbon. Tom stared at it for a few moments. He didn't need to be told whose it was. It was Emily's. He knew he had to get back to the army camp as quickly as possible.

CHAPTER 12

The following morning Tom rode up to the army camp.

'I've got an urgent message for the major,' he told the guard at the gate.

The way Tom had galloped up to the gate and his dishevelled state left the gatekeeper in no doubt about the urgency of the message. Five minutes later he was shown into the major's study.

'Is it about Emily?' demanded the major.

'Yes. She's been kidnapped by the Apaches.'

'Oh, no!' There was a pause while the major recovered from the shock. He waved Tom to a chair. 'You'd better give me the full story,' he said.

Tom explained how Luis and his outlaws had stolen the gold. How he and Emily had been forced to go with them. How they had ended up in the outlaws' camp. Then, while he was away, Apaches had seized the gold. They had also seized Emily.

'Then she's still alive,' declared the major, with hope in his voice.

'As far as I know. There's this character named Carlos. He swears that he saw an Apache ride off with her.'

'Pour a couple of drinks, while I think this one out.'

Tom poured two generous glasses of whiskey. 'So the Apaches have got the gold,' commented the major. 'You know what this means?'

'That they will use it to get guns,' Tom finished the thought.

'Exactly. Almost a hundred bars of gold will buy a lot of guns.'

Tom had almost emptied his glass. The major indicated to him to pour another for himself.

'If the Apaches can get, say, a couple of hundred more guns, then they will be joined by other Apaches,' the major pointed out.

'Exactly,' said Tom. 'And their first target will be this camp, since we are nearest to the border. There will be a bloodbath which will make Custer's fight against the Sioux and Cheyenne seem like a tea party.'

'I don't agree with your choice of words,' said the major, as he poured himself another drink. 'But it could certainly be on the same scale as Custer's last stand.'

'We've got one chance,' said Tom. 'We've got to attack them before they can go ahead and shop for guns.'

'Do you know where their camp is?'

Tom explained that Carlos would act as a guide to take them there.

'I suppose he'd want payment for it,' suggested the major.

'No, he said that after he had seen what the Apaches had done to the Mexican women and children he'd gladly take us there without any payment.'

'Right.' The major became businesslike. 'I assume you've thought out a plan to attack the Apache camp.'

'Yes. I'd want a platoon of men. At least thirty. We could ride to Luis's camp. If we start in an hour's time we could arrive there before sunset. We rest in the camp. Then we start at first light and should arrive in the Apache camp at some time in the afternoon. We should be able to take them by surprise. I'd like to give them the same treatment they gave to Luis and his outlaws.'

'You don't kill the women and children. That's an order,' said the major, noting the anger in Tom's voice.

Tom took a deep breath. 'All right. But if they've harmed Emily, I swear I won't be responsible for my actions.'

'Right, we'll see about getting this mission organized,' stated the major. He called in a sergeant and started giving him orders. The sergeant's face registered surprise. He was even more surprised when he was told that Tom would be in charge.

'You and your men will be under the command of Sergeant Benson,' said the major.

'Captain Benson,' said Tom.

The sergeant was dumbfounded. He had never heard anyone contradict the major before.

'You drive a hard bargain, Tom,' said the major. 'All right. Captain Benson.'

In a matter of minutes, the camp was in turmoil. Orders were shouted. Horses were given a hasty meal. Tom, too, managed to grab some food.

After having a quick wash and a shave he made his way to the room where the uniforms were kept. The corporal in charge had already been given the order that Tom was to be given his old captain's uniform.

'I've kept it brushed and shone the buttons, sir,' said the corporal, with a smile.

'Thanks,' said Tom.

'Don't forget your sword,' said the corporal, as he handed Tom the weapon.

There was one other gift that Tom was to receive before he set out. It was always the tradition of the camp that the cavalrymen would receive a ribbon from their loved ones and pin them on their tunic before riding off.

Tom had put on his uniform when Emily's aunt knocked and came into the room. Tom was holding the ribbon he had brought from the outlaw's camp, undecided what to do.

'Here, let me pin it on for you, Tom,' said Aunt Matilda. 'I know it's Emily's. I bought it for her. Promise me one thing, will you?' she said with a sob.

'What is it?'

'That you will bring her back alive. I don't care if she is a squaw woman.'

The cavalrymen rode out of the camp. It was a heart-warming sight. They sang their traditional song as they went. 'The Girl I Left Behind Me.'

The hours sad I left a maid
A lingering farewell taking
Whose sighs and tears my steps delayed;
I thought her heart was breaking.
In hurried words her name I blest:

I breathed the vows that bind me.
And to my heart in anguish pressed
The girl I left behind me.

Well *he* wasn't leaving a girl behind him. Most of the cavalrymen had left wives or sweethearts behind, but not Tom Benson. He was hoping against hope that there would be a girlfriend waiting for him. If she were alive, that would mean everything to him. He had heard the word 'squaw woman' bandied about in the mess. If the worse came to the worst and she had been forced to become a squaw woman, he could still love her. After all, he had married a Mexican, Carlotta, and the other officers had laid bets on how long they had thought the marriage would last. Well, it had lasted until her tragic end. And it had been a happy marriage. There was no reason why, even if Emily had become 'soiled goods', their future shouldn't be a happy one.

The fact that the Apache had ridden off with her and she was alive had given him hope. He had seen what the other Apaches had done to the Mexican women in the camp. According to Carlos, Emily had been alive when she had been abducted. He clung to that thought with a desperate single-mindedness as they rode through the desert.

They reached Luis's camp just as darkness was approaching. To Tom's relief, Carlos came to meet them. They dismounted and Tom introduced him to the sergeant.

'So this is where the massacre took place,' said the sergeant. He was looking around as if expecting to see some evidence of the carnage.

'I moved all the bodies,' explained Carlos. 'There is a convenient pit a few hundred yards away from the camp. I've put them all in there. If you want to see them, sergeant, I will take you there while it is still light.'

'No, thanks,' said the sergeant, hurriedly. 'I accept your word.'

Tom told the men to have their food. While the men set about lighting a few fires and warming their beans, Tom sat down with Carlos.

'I want you to tell me exactly the lie of the land of this Apache camp,' Tom ordered.

'It's in a slight hollow. As I said, about a day's ride away.'

'So they won't be able to see us as we approach?'

'There are usually one or two guards here.' Carlos drew a circle in the soft earth with a stick. Then he placed two crosses a short distance away.

'So if we can get rid of the guards we should have a free ride into the camp,' said Tom, thoughtfully.

'That's right. Carlos can guarantee that.'

Their meal of beans and bread arrived.

'Eat up,' said Tom. 'We'll be starting early in the morning.'

They started at first light. Carlos was riding alongside Tom. The men knew they had a long ride ahead of them before they reached the Apache camp, but they were all used to riding for hours without a halt.

Tom was relieved that the terrain wasn't too much of a problem. He had feared that they might have to ride up and down valleys which would slow them down considerably. But in fact the land was reasonably flat and so they were able to make good time.

Another thing in their favour was that it was cooler up on the mountain. If they had been riding on the plain below it would soon have become unbearably hot. But the fact that they were several thousand feet high meant that riding was quite pleasant.

They had been riding for about three hours when Carlos raised a warning hand.

'We're getting nearer,' he informed Tom.

So much for Carlos's forecast of a day's ride, thought Tom. Still it was a big advantage for the men to have arrived at the camp in just a few hours. It meant that they would be going into battle still comparatively fresh.

He gave the order for the men to dismount. He told the sergeant, whose name was Wilson, that he and Carlos were going forward to investigate the situation. If anything should happen to him then he, Wilson, would be in charge.

Carlos led Tom to a ridge. Carlos flung himself on the ground. Tom copied his action.

The reason for Carlos's unexpected movement lay a couple of hundred feet ahead. It took the shape of a solitary Apache, who was standing near a tree. Fortunately he wasn't looking in their direction. He was looking back at the hollow behind him where the smoke from the tepees told Tom that it was the Apache camp.

Tom held up one finger to indicate that there was only one guard. Carlos nodded.

Tom knew that he had to get across a hundred yards of open terrain and hope that the Apache wouldn't turn round before he reached him. He took off his sword. Carlos watched him while he produced a long knife. It was the standard army knife, which, apart from being useful for skinning rabbits and chopping heads off chickens, could also be a useful weapon in a close fight.

Tom nodded to Carlos to indicate that he was about to set off. He suited his action to the sign. He stood up and started to sprint across the intervening distance.

His eyes were glued on the Apache. He was getting nearer. Fifty yards. Twenty yards. Ten yards. At that moment the Apache turned. He must have heard a slight sound from the rapidly approaching Tom. He too drew his knife.

The Apache's lips were bared in eager anticipation as the two men faced each other.

The Apache lunged and Tom was just in time to side-step. Even so the Apache's knife cut away a piece of Tom's sleeve.

Tom knew he had to act quickly. The Apache was a dangerous opponent. The next time it wouldn't be Tom's sleeve but his arm that the Apache could slice.

The Apache was waiting for Tom's next move so that he could counter-attack. If anything his grin was wider. They stood facing each other only three feet apart. Suddenly Tom made his move. He kicked the Apache in the crotch. The Apache, who had been expecting a move by Tom's knife, was taken completely by surprise. Not only was Tom's move unexpected but the result was spectacular. A size twelve army boot delivered from a fourteen-stone man had its desired effect. The Apache doubled up with pain. He dropped his knife. Tom didn't hesitate. His own knife unerringly found the Apache's heart.

Tom returned to his waiting men.

'Right. Let's go,' he said. 'We don't kill the women and children. But we don't take any prisoners.'

The attack was a complete success. The Apaches were completely unprepared. Many of them were shot by the cavalrymen as they emerged from the tepees. The ones that survived the first attack were mercilessly cut down by the soldiers' swords as they frantically tried to find some weapons to defend themselves.

Tom was in the thick of the battle, shouting encouragement to his men. As he thrust and cut with his sword he kept looking around, searching for a special face, but when the battle was over there had still been no sign of Emily. Maybe she had been killed after all. Even in the euphoria of winning the battle his heart sank.

An Indian squaw who was standing near his horse said, 'Thank you for rescuing me, Tom.'

It couldn't be! Tom stared at her in disbelief. Her hair had been braided round her head. She was wearing a loose fitting dress and moccasins. On her face she had red dye on her cheeks.

'It isn't–' he gasped.

'I thought you would have recognized your future bride,' Emily teased.

'But–' For the second time Tom was at a loss for words. He had jumped down from his horse. He took the only course of action open to him. He kissed her.

The soldiers gave a cheer at the action.

When he released her she whispered something in his ear. Even though she whispered quietly a couple of the men heard her. She had said, 'I'm still a virgin.'

A quarter of an hour later she had untied her hair and let it flow down her back. She had also washed as much of the red dye from her face as possible. Tom had given the order for each soldier to carry three bars of gold in their saddle-bags. They set off back to the outlaws' camp.

Emily was riding behind Tom. 'I'll have a story to tell our children, when I tell them bedtime stories,' she said. 'I'll tell them how I was captured by some Mexican outlaws. Then I was captured by some Apaches. But I was rescued by a handsome army captain. It's nice to see you've got your rank back,' she added.

'What about the Indian who rescued you? Why didn't he have his way with you?'

'That's another story,' she said. 'It turned out that he didn't like women. He was the chief's son and so was supposed to take a bride. Obviously he didn't fancy any of the Apache women, but he thought that by capturing me he could pretend that he was a real man. In fact I spent an interesting couple of days learning Apache. I even learned the Apache for, "It's your turn to kill a pig".'

The soldiers behind couldn't understand why Tom and Emily were laughing their heads off as they rode along.

The publishers hope that this book has given you enjoyable reading. Large Print Books are especially designed to be as easy to see and hold as possible. If you wish a complete list of our books please ask at your local library or write directly to:

Dales Large Print Books
Magna House, Long Preston,
Skipton, North Yorkshire.
BD23 4ND

1	2	3	4	5	6	7	8	9	10
11	12	13	14	15	16	17	18	19	20
21	22	23	24	25	26	27	28	29	30
31	32	33	34	35	36	37	38	39	40
41	42	43	44	45	46	47	48	49	50
51	52	53	54	55	56	57	58	59	60
61	62	63	64	65	66	67	68	69	70
71	72	73	74	75	76	77	78	79	80
81	82	83	84	85	86	87	88	89	90
91	92	93	94	95	96	97	98	99	100
101	102	103	104	105	106	107	108	109	110
111	112	113	114	115	116	117	118	119	120
121	122	123	124	125	126	127	128	129	130
131	132	133	134	135	136	137	138	139	140
141	142	143	144	145	146	147	148	149	150
151	152	153	154	155	156	157	158	159	160
161	162	163	164	165	166	167	168	169	170
171	172	173	174	175	176	177	178	179	180
181	182	183	184	185	186	187	188	189	190
191	192	193	194	195	196	197	198	199	200
201	202	203	204	205	206	207	208	209	210
211	212	213	214	215	216	217	218	219	220
221	222	223	224	225	226	227	228	229	230
231	232	233	234	235	236	237	238	239	240
241	242	243	244	245	246	247	248	249	250
251	252	253	254	255	256	257	258	259	260
261	262	263	264	265	266	267	268	269	270
271	272	273	274	275	276	277	278	279	280
281	282	283	284	285	286	287	288	289	290
291	292	293	294	295	296	297	298	299	300
301	302	303	304	305	306	307	308	309	310
311	312	313	314	315	316	317	318	319	320
321	322	323	324	325	326	327	328	329	330
331	332	333	334	335	336	337	338	339	340
341	342	343	344	345	346	347	348	349	350
351	352	353	354	355	356	357	358	359	360
361	362	363	364	365	366	367	368	369	370
371	372	373	374	375	376	377	378	379	380
381	382	383	384	385	386	387	388	389	390
391	392	393	394	395	396	397	398	399	400